LIKE A CHAMPION

STORIES

VINCENT CHU

7.13 BOOKS

"Chu finds ways to turn the everyday into the revelatory… He covers a host of relationships – familial, romantic, occupational – and, in doing so, showcases the complexities of the characters on display. Chu's stories are solidly realistic in their scope, exploring everyday issues with charm and empathy – and occasional moments of unexpected humor"
Kirkus Reviews

"Vincent Chu takes us on a journey through real life, with brief glimpses into the lives of diverse characters. While each character and story is different, there is something relatable about them all. You'll find yourself among friends in these stories"
San Francisco Book Review

"*Like a Champion* is a lighthearted testimony to life's unexpected turns… Chu creates a context where the lonely feel loved, connections thrive through conflicts, and private issues unfold in public spaces. Above all, each story retains a sense of hope or new beginning"
Forth Magazine

"With gentle precision, Chu moves beyond the writerly adage of show don't tell; he doesn't want the reader to be shown or told anything, rather asking the reader to experience the feeling of being sucked into another person's head… by the end of the book, we're not just cheering for his characters, but for Chu himself"
East Bay Review

© 2018, Vincent Chu.

Printed and distributed by 7.13 Books. First paperback edition, first printing: February 28, 2018

Cover design: Verena Herbst
Author photo: Henriette Kriese

ISBN-10: 0-9984092-6-X
ISBN-13: 978-0-9984092-6-9

Library of Congress Control Number: 2017956193

This collection is available in a variety of electronic formats including EPUB for mobile devices, MOBI for Kindles, and PDFs for American and European laser printers.

www.713books.com

Contents

FRED FROM FINANCE

Fred wanted to be more likeable in the office. That was something they never told you growing up. That being likeable was a hell of a lot more valuable for your future than math or history. Maybe it couldn't be learned in school. Oh, that would be a shame, thought Fred. Maybe humans were born likeable or not. Maybe at Pear Tree Industries and corporations all around the world, employees were naturally divided into haves and have nots. Have likeability. Have not.

Take Glen. Damn, that guy was likeable. Confident, warm, full of compliments, full head of hair. When you talked to that man, you felt better about yourself. Fred sometimes wondered how people felt when they talked to him. Uncomfortable? Depressed?

People liked Glen and it showed. Last month on Glen's Facebook page, seventy people wished him a happy birthday. Seventy! Fred didn't know seventy people. Fred and Glen weren't friends on Facebook but Glen kept his profile public. What a guy. Glen even got birthday wishes on his LinkedIn page. Offline, he also got balloons, cake from the VP, and of course, a happy hour. Fred didn't go, but he heard things.

It was only 11:30. Still early, thought Fred. Plenty of time for his own surprise birthday lunch to transpire. He brought leftover pasta anyway, something he could eat today or tomorrow in case something came up.

After lunch, Fred worked on old reports. He was pretty full from his pasta. Food coma is what Glen had called the feeling once in the elevator after a client meeting. Fred often ate too much leftover pasta for lunch. It didn't make sense to cook one serving, you had to make the whole pot.

At 3:15, Fred got the call from Zoe in Human Resources. It was about time, thought Fred. Of course. HR was probably the birthday celebration task force and Zoe the team lead. Which made sense. People respected Zoe. She came from a bigger company, one that really had their stuff together, and everyone kept mind of that. She dressed professional but fashionable, sometimes even wearing skirts above the knees on Fridays.

"Have a seat, Fred," said Zoe as Fred entered her compact office. There was a miniature Zen garden on her desk next to a photo of her husband and adorable baby boy. The closet door was closed. Fred imagined four or five co-workers could fit in there. "Surprise!" they would all shout, leaping out when he least expected, holding a cake, carrot, his favorite. Amir from Accounts Payable would be in there, Laney from Legal, perhaps those fun and crazy IT guys—

"Fred? Are you even listening?" asked Zoe.

"Sorry. Food coma," said Fred with a soft smile.

"This should come as little shock, Fred, but we have to let you go. Since your review in June, we haven't seen any improvement in the areas we very specifically addressed. In fact, your performance has declined. We'll take this time to reconsider the position and see whether Tuan can handle the full workload in Finance. In this folder you'll find everything you need. Marley will escort you out of the building in thirty minutes. Are there any questions from your side?" The way Zoe stared at Fred, he thought asking a question seemed inappropriate.

Waiting for the elevator, Fred looked at the folder. On the cover, an ethnically ambiguous woman gazed out courageously at sailboats on a horizon. It wasn't Zoe's fault. She was just doing her job. She had a family, after all. A baby. Fred could actually admire how Zoe handled the situation. Direct. Professional. It would be unfair to call her a cold-hearted cyborg or spineless corporate pawn. Could she have been kinder? Sure. Could she have displayed more compassion? You bet your ass. But that's business these days, thought Fred.

Someone like Glen? He might have done things differently. He might have cursed senior management for their shortsightedness, recommended an old recruiter friend, applauded all the years of dignified and respectable work—

"Hey there, Fred. How are you holding up? Doing a little better this week?"

Fred looked up. Had he and Glen talked last week?

"Hi, Glen," said Fred as he got inside the elevator. "Two, please."

"Today has been one of those days," said Glen. "I'm sure I don't have to tell you. All ready for the weekend?"

"Today's my last day."

"Brother." Glen stopped and looked Fred in the eyes. "Congratulations. Going to greener pastures I'm sure, smart guy like you. This place can never retain good talent for very long."

"Well, nine years," said Fred.

"Celebrating big tonight, I bet," said Glen.

"I should get home and start updating my resume."

"Seriously?"

"Why put off until tomorrow… "

"Your work ethic is inspiring. But come on, your last day?"

"It's my birthday, too."

Glen let out a good laugh. "You certainly know how to plan an exit, I'll give you that. Hey Fred, I've got an idea. How about you let me buy you a drink?"

Did Glen say a drink?

"I need to leave the building," said Fred.

"The Lemon Leaf. One hour. I'll wrangle up some of the guys, we can throw you a proper going-away happy hour."

Some of the guys? Going-away happy hour? That was almost better than a birthday happy hour. No, it was definitely better. People had fewer going-aways in life than birthdays.

"Could you invite Amir from Accounts Payable, Laney from Legal, maybe even those fun and crazy IT guys?"

"It's your special day, Fred."

"Yes," said Fred. "I suppose you're right."

"See you at the bar, buddy," said Glen.

Glen shook Fred's hand before getting out of the elevator. The handshake was firm but friendly, warm but definitely not sweaty. What a guy. Fred was already starting to feel better.

By the time Fred cleared his desk and loaded up his plastic milk crate, it was time to leave the building. There wasn't much chance to say goodbye to anyone. It was okay. Fred would see everyone at the happy hour.

Marley waited patiently while Fred packed.

Marley was built like the old HP printer scanner down in the mailroom, heavy and indestructible. He used to work in Shipping until six months ago when he was promoted to Building Management.

Marley escorted Fred down to the parking lot and

helped Fred load the box into the trunk of his Kia, even though that wasn't his job and the crate wasn't very heavy.

"Hey Fred, do me a favor," said Marley as he rested his heavy hand on Fred's shoulder. "Keep your head up, okay man?"

Fred chirped his alarm and started walking down the street. The Lemon Leaf was just a few blocks away.

Lately, Fred had been thinking a lot about how he ended up here, at this point, in the universe. What were the events in life that led him to become a Finance Manager at Pear Tree Industries and remain so for a decade? Fred was a people person deep down. Always had been. He liked people. He loved people. He just didn't really interact with them that much, and that's why most people probably didn't know this about him.

Fred kicked a rock as he turned the corner. It bounced off the curb and hit a car.

Where had things gone wrong? When Fred was a kid, he had a Care Bears calculator. That must have started it all. In the third grade, he scored high on a standardized test. That put him in the "Gifted and Talented" program. That made his father proud. His son, the chubby kid with few friends and poor hand-eye coordination, was finally good at something. AP Calculus came senior year. Then acceptance into the top finance program in the state. After graduation, what was Fred to do? Start a job in finance naturally.

It was 5:30. Happy hour had already started when Fred walked into the Lemon Leaf and went to the bar. The place was plain and bare, the cactus in the corner and bandannas on the chairs suggested a Tex-Mex theme. It reminded him of the office a few years ago when they had their Cinco de Mayo celebration.

"Be right with you, tweed," said a passing bartender.

It was tragic, thought Fred as he took off his jacket. A born people person like him stuck crunching numbers in a cubicle all day. Whose performance wouldn't decline under the weight of such a realization?

The bartender returned. "This is the Lemon Leaf and they call me Gertrude. What are you having?"

Gertrude the bartender was not very charming, Fred was afraid to admit. She was sort of pretty, when you got past the fact that she had no color or expression in her face, her voice seemed unnecessarily loud, and she dressed rather frumpy for someone in the service industry, in Fred's humble opinion. But of course, nobody asked for his humble opinion. In fact, why was Fred criticizing this complete stranger? Would Glen do that? Come to think of it, what was this woman Gertrude thinking about *Fred* at the moment?

Fred sucked in his gut and moved a few strands of hair. Did his breath still smell from lunch?

"One beer, please. Wait." Fred picked up the happy hour card. "One Zombie Punch."

"You have exquisite taste," said Gertrude.

"Oh, and I'm hosting a happy hour," said Fred. "Actually, I'm being thrown a happy hour, by my colleagues. Today was my last day at work. And it's my birthday, too. I'm just the first one here."

"I'm extremely happy for you," said Gertrude.

"Do I need to reserve a table?" asked Fred.

"No."

"Are you sure?"

Gertrude looked around the empty bar. "Not usually in life but today, yes."

"What if twenty people come?"

"One can only imagine."

Fred thought about this as Gertrude put away her pen.

"I'll make you a deal," said Gertrude. "What's your name?"

"Fred."

"When your party arrives, Fred, I'll upgrade you to our special corporate events table by the clean window. Until then, sit tight. I was up late watching a *Happy Days* marathon and I don't want to run around any more than I have to today."

Gertrude came back with one Zombie Punch.

Fred drank. He was thirsty from the walk.

So what would Fred talk about when the guys got there? Should he prepare some sort of farewell speech? Acknowledge the strong relationships he'd formed over the years, celebrate the friendships that would last well into the future? Fred always hated public speaking. Opening up in front of others, sharing what was on his mind.

His sister Lisa was the outgoing one. But now that Fred was an uncle, he figured he should get better at public speaking. Kids tended to like adults who were confident and comfortable speaking in front of others. Women seemed to like that kind of thing, too. Maybe that's why he'd been single since Genie, and perhaps why he and Genie hadn't worked out in the first place, and possibly why he didn't have any children of his own when some men his age had one or two.

Fred finished his drink and waved to Gertrude for a second.

There were books on how to be better with people. Fred could learn it. His roommate from college was into that type of stuff. Tony Robbins, *Rich Dad Poor Dad*, *The Pickup Artist*, how to make a girl go home with you in 20 minutes. Wouldn't that be quite a skill. Wait. That was creepy. Pathetic. Guys like Glen were naturally likeable, and that was the difference. That made all the difference in the world. Did that mean Fred had no chance? No, thought Fred. He just had to work a little harder at it. And he would.

He looked at his watch. 6:15. It was always hard to wrap up loose ends on a Friday.

Gertrude arrived with another glass. "Zombie for the suit."

"What's in these?" asked Fred.

"Can I ask you something?" asked Gertrude.

"I guess so, sure."

"I made a bet with my coworker about you."

"A bet about me?"

"Did you quit or get fired?"

"Excuse me?"

"You said it was your last day today."

"Oh, it's not important."

"Where did you work?"

"Just an office somewhere."

"Somewhere where?" asked Gertrude.

"Somewhere nearby," said Fred.

Gertrude leaned in and studied Fred's face. "You got fired." She began restacking the coasters. "On your birthday too, wow. I worked at an office once. Marketing coordinator at a carpet company. The worst years of my life. Crap boss, uneasy vibe all the time. But now I tolerate my job. The money's decent and I get to meet interesting human beings, talk to them even, every single day. Not a bad deal, right?"

Fred nodded, thinking. "Not bad at all."

"Please use a coaster," said Gertrude, looking at the puddle of condensation in front of Fred.

Fred watched Gertrude go into the kitchen. The more Fred thought about it, losing his job was probably a good thing. After all, who knew what opportunities were in store for him? Maybe corporate America wasn't right for him. Vincent Van Gogh didn't start painting until his late twenties. Yes, Fred could be anything he wanted to be in life. A taxidermist, a street performer, a soup kitchen chef, a Hollywood casting agent, a comedian! Imagine that, making people laugh for a living. That would be a rewarding profession.

Fred looked at his watch again. Did he ever stay past seven on a Friday? He couldn't remember. He waved to Gertrude for another.

Anyway, Fred had to be realistic. He had a niece to think about, he shouldn't forget. Little Baylee couldn't grow up with nice toys and cool clothes and go to college with an uncle who performed street magic on the promenade for spare change. Not to mention the single-parent household Baylee was going to grow up in. Oh, how dare he say that. Lisa was terrific. Strong. Admirable. But it was his responsibility, his duty, as a good uncle, to provide some kind of financial support. Not to mention one day Fred wanted a family of his own. Sure, why not? And he certainly wouldn't be able to find a wife or finance a home or buy the good baby food with crumpled-up bills in a dusty top hat. Where the hell was everyone anyway?

Gertrude came with another Zombie Punch.

"Gertrude, when does happy hour end?" asked Fred.

Gertrude looked at her watch then walked over to the bar. She rang a small brass bell. "One minute ago!"

It was 8:01.

Happy hour was over.

Who was Fred kidding.

Fred lowered his head and focused on his drink.

Seriously. Happy hour? The guys? Nobody was coming. Not Amir. Not Laney. Not those fun and crazy IT guys.

And certainly not Glen.

Glen. You know what? thought Fred. Glen was a fake. That's right. Fake as hell. It dawned on Fred. To be likeable you had to be fake. There were no two ways around it. How could you be appealing to so many different people? You had to act *differently* with each one of them. And that meant being fake. A phony. Not your true self. Fred couldn't believe that he had actually wanted to be like Glen just a few hours ago. No, Glen was the exact opposite of who Fred wanted to be. Glen was just a lying, gutless, Propecia-popping, Jeep-driving, conference-call-dialing-in, good-for-nothing piece of shit.

Yes, that's just what Glen was.

In fact, if Fred ever saw Glen again he would give him a piece of his mind. Fred would let it all out. He would explain to Glen that he saw right through his disgusting act. Glen might have had the office fooled, and those seventy people who wished him a happy birthday on Facebook fooled, but Fred was no fool. No way. Fred knew the ugly truth. Glen was just a bad person faking to be a good person so that people would like him more. Hell, maybe a lot of people in the world did this. Fred twisted his napkin until it turned into a little churro.

"Earth to Fred." Gertrude dropped two shots onto the table and stood beside them.

"Sorry?" said Fred.

"Happy birthday," said Gertrude.

"Those aren't mine."

"They're on the house."

"Who's that one for?"

"I can't let you drink alone on your birthday, it's company policy."

"Company policy?"

"Friday is the worst day for happy hours," said Gertrude, sitting down. "People tend to skip out on work obligations and start their weekends early. Anyway, you don't want to be hanging out with work people on a Friday. You're better than that, Fred."

"Maybe you're right," said Fred.

"Less talking and more drinking," said Gertrude.

They drank. It was rum.

"You know who liked rum?" asked Fred, grimacing. "George Washington."

Gertrude laughed. "You're alright, Fred. I hope you come back again one day. Maybe you can even tell me the story of how you got fired."

Gertrude put her hand on Fred's wrist and managed a version of a smile. Then she abruptly removed her hand, stood and took away the empty shot glasses before Fred could say anything.

Gertrude looked much better when she smiled. But was she smiling at Fred or was she smiling because of the rum? Oh, it didn't matter. At least Fred got to drink with someone on his birthday.

Fred took out his wallet to pay. When he opened it, a piece of plastic fell out. He picked it up and looked at it. It was his employee key card. The one that opened all the doors at Pear Tree Industries. The consummate professional Zoe, all stone-faced and noble, had forgotten to take his employee key card. Fred still had access to the building.

This was incredible.

It was dark when Fred began walking back to the office. He felt giddy, giddier than he'd felt in years. He was grinning. Fred had never been so eager to get inside the walls of Pear Tree Industries. As he walked along the side of the road, headlights floated past him in the night air as ideas began to take shape in his head. Having this key card was a unique opportunity few humans were given in life.

The possibilities were infinite. Fred could walk into Glen's office and rip down all of his stupid training certifications and regional sales awards. He could draw a Hitler mustache on that one photo of him and the VP fishing in Cancun, draw a penis on that photo of him and his fiancé posing by the Leaning Tower of Pisa. Then

Fred could go into Zoe's office and take a big leak right in her miniature Zen garden. What a spiritual awakening that would be! Or Fred could keep it simple and toilet paper the place. He could even write his name in Sharpie on the brand new reception wall. *"Sincerely yours, Fred from Finance."* Why the hell not? Fred didn't give a damn what anybody there thought about him.

At the offices of Pear Tree Industries, only the entrance lights were still on. For some reason Fred felt lightheaded when he arrived. The walk back from the Lemon Leaf seemed to take longer than the walk there. Before going inside, Fred decided he should rest.

Fred opened the door to his Kia, parked in front, and sat inside. This would give him a chance to catch his breath and refine his strategy. Once Fred closed the door, he could hear himself breathe for the first time all day. The air was clean and sweet smelling. The plastic on the dash was cool to the touch. Fred had forgotten to close one of his windows.

Just then, the building's entrance doors made a bang and two people walked out. Fred panicked and dropped down. He tilted his seat back with the tiny lever.

Who was leaving the office at this hour?

Fred lifted his head just above the wheel, squinting.

The lights by the entrance were bright.

The legs of the women were tanned and glowing. The shoulders of the man were broad and filled out his shirt.

The two figures shifted positions.

It was Glen and Zoe.

Glen and Zoe did not work together. In fact, Fred couldn't recall ever seeing them speak to each other in the office. So what were they doing leaving together so late? Perhaps it was a coincidence.

But it didn't seem like one. They were standing rather close. Actually, they were almost touching. As a matter of fact, they were definitely touching. They were kissing. Wait a minute. Yes, Glen and Zoe were kissing.

Fred fumbled for his phone. He got it out and sat all the way up. He began tapping. Chick. Chick. Chick. Chick. He looked at the photos. A photographer for *National Geographic*, perhaps that was another career he could pursue. Clear as day. Glen and Zoe were kissing. It was them, without a shadow of a doubt.

This was too good to be true. It was better than having a key card to the office. Holy crap.

Glen was engaged to be married! Zoe had a family, a new baby boy for Christ's sake. Fred started to despise Glen even more than before, and Zoe now, too. How could two adults, two professionals, act so recklessly and selfishly? How could they put their loved ones, everything they had going in their perfect lives, at risk? And for what? Some cheap and temporary office fling? What the hell were they thinking?

Fred slithered back down into position and reexamined the photos. His creative juices began to flow.

What could Fred do with these photos?

He could use them as blackmail, but for what purpose? Well, he could take them directly to HR, but then again Zoe worked in HR. He could post them somewhere. Like Facebook. Sure. That's exactly what social media was made for. *"Happy belated birthday, Glen. Just wanted to share this nice picture of you and Zoe from the office to brighten up your day. LOL!"* No, hold on. That was a little crazy. Evil even. That would make things a hell of a lot worse for Glen and Zoe. A thousand times worse.

But maybe they deserved it, thought Fred.

Glen and Zoe turned and walked right toward Fred's Kia. Fred dropped back down. He laid his body over the middle console and pressed his cheek against the cushion of his passenger seat, remaining still, sucking in his own hot Zombie breath.

His two former colleagues walked past. Fred could hear them talking and soon they sounded far enough away again. He sat back up. Glen and Zoe were now standing by Glen's red Cherokee at the end of the aisle.

Fred got in a comfortable position and resumed watching. But at a closer distance now, he was able to notice something. But what was it? It was Zoe.

Zoe wasn't smiling or laughing. No, she wasn't. Zoe was crying. And Glen didn't look happy or flirty. He looked sad. Sad as hell. Had Fred missed something?

Fred opened the pictures on his phone and zoomed in

on their faces. Zoe was crying then, too. It was not a sexy face she had been making earlier as Fred assumed but a quite miserable-looking one. And Glen looked similarly in pain, eyes red, jaw clenched like he couldn't speak. Fred had never seen Glen look like that.

What was going on? Come to think of it, Zoe and Glen had seemed off the past few months. Zoe was a lot quieter since she came back from maternity leave. She rarely came out of her office these days. Was it just the newborn baby? Or was it possible? Was it Glen's baby? Stop it, thought Fred. Pure conjecture. Throw that out. Well actually, Glen had been engaged for over three years which is pretty long. And lately Janice never came by the office. She used to visit every Friday. Did anyone ever ask Glen why? Or how Glen was doing in general? Glen was always asking everyone else about their weekends and kids' soccer games and latest project wins, but did people return the favor?

Zoe, too. People came to her with their problems, but did anyone ever ask the Head of HR about her problems? How she was doing? Maybe that wasn't allowed in the employee handbook.

Fred continued watching as Zoe handed Glen a folded envelope placed on top of a grey gym t-shirt. Zoe looked at Glen, said something Fred couldn't hear, then wiped her cheek and went away toward her silver Audi. Glen stood watching, motionless like the cars around him.

Glen waited until Zoe got inside her Audi before he got

into his Jeep. Zoe started her engine and reversed out of her parking spot. Soon Glen did the same. Zoe drove left out of the parking lot. Shortly after, Glen drove right out of the parking lot. They both disappeared into the night.

Fred looked down at the pictures on his phone.

What was he doing. Fred didn't work at Pear Tree Industries anymore. He wasn't even supposed to be there. And he had nothing better to do, on his birthday, than this.

Fred took a deep breath.

He went through his camera gallery and looked at each picture of Zoe and Glen. There must have been more than twenty photos. He carefully deleted each one.

What about his key card? Well, he could leave that in the delivery drop box outside of the entrance doors. That should be fine. Hopefully Zoe wouldn't get in trouble or anything for forgetting about it. And he still had access to his email for a few more hours, he remembered. Maybe he should write a farewell email to everyone when he got home. That would be the right thing to do, thought Fred.

There was a loud knock on the glass. Fred dropped his phone. He looked up.

It was Marley.

Fred rolled down the window.

"Fred?" said Marley. "I thought that was you."

"Hi, Marley," said Fred. "It's me."

"Shoot, I was sure I'd be the last one here today. What the hell are you doing? You were supposed to leave hours ago."

"My key card. They forgot to take my key card, so I just wanted to return it."

"Well, that's no big deal. I can take that for you." Marley took the key card from Fred through the window.

"I guess I'll be heading home," said Fred. "Have a good night, Marley."

"Hold on just a minute, Fred. You know I've got to ask," said Marley. "Have you been drinking?"

"Today's my birthday."

"No kidding? Happy birthday, man. Damn Fred, what do you call a company that fires a fellow on his birthday then has him escorted out of the building like some criminal? Pear Tree Industries."

Fred smiled. "They're not so bad. I owe a lot to this place, I guess."

"Like hell you do," said Marley. "You're talented, Fred. A talented guy. Smart. Good with people. Don't worry, you'll be back on your feet in no time."

"I was thinking about taking a break from the corporate thing," said Fred.

"Why not," said Marley. "What are you going to do?"

"I don't really know yet," said Fred.

"I always wanted to be a marine biologist."

"That sounds interesting."

"But I can't swim."

"Do you need to know how to swim to be a marine biologist?"

"I don't know, actually."

"Marley, you think I'm good with people?"

"Good how?"

"You said a second ago you thought I was good with people," said Fred.

"Oh, yeah. I do, Fred. Sure," said Marley. "I think you don't always show it, so it's not obvious. But I mean, I like you. You just got to open up more, man. Give a little to get a little. Know what I'm trying to say? Treat people how you wished they treated you, start with that and you'll get along with people fine. It's not rocket science."

"I suppose it's not," said Fred.

"But shit, that's just one man's opinion," said Marley. "Let me call you a taxi, I can't let you drive home like this."

"Marley, you want to hear a joke?"

"What do you mean?"

"A joke, something funny."

"From you?"

Fred shrugged.

Marley stared at Fred, skeptical.

"Okay," said Fred. "Let's see. What did the baby computer say to his father?"

"I'm sure I have no idea," said Marley.

"*Data*," said Fred.

It was silent then Marley sighed.

"Fred," said Marley. "Now, I know you're drunk."

"I didn't tell it right," said Fred.

"Promise me, never tell that joke to anyone again."

Marley laughed and so did Fred.

The sound carried across the parking lot.

"It's getting late," said Fred. "I won't keep you much longer. I'm sure you have plans tonight with the family."

"Me? Not really," said Marley. "Tell you the truth, me and the wife have been fighting like cats and dogs lately, not to mention the in-laws are coming to visit and the water heater is broken, plus the kids still aren't talking to me because of the whole birthday party thing. On days like today, I try not to get home too early."

"I'm sorry to hear that."

"What do I have to complain about?"

"It could be worse."

"Exactly."

"You could lose your job," said Fred.

"There's that," said Marley. He laughed and took out his pack of Newports. He pulled out a cigarette and lit it with a small plastic lighter then put the pack and lighter back into his shirt pocket. "Say Fred, you want to have a beer?"

"A beer?"

"With me, a beer."

Fred looked up at Marley.

"After all, it is still Friday night," said Marley, breathing in. "And I believe it is still your birthday."

Fred turned back toward the office.

"Come on," said Marley as he opened the driver's side door and extended Fred his hand. "Out of the car. I know a funny little place nearby we can walk to."

BOOM TOWN

arlotta would kill him. Quite soon in fact. She would leap up during this next burpee and jerk her size-five Adidas forward and kick him right in his boulder face, his face like those jagged Pebble Beach cliffs you see when golf is on TV, first toe, then heel, a clean swoop. One two. Or not one two. One two *three*, toe hit, heel hit, Manfred hit the floor. Bam. Combo. A new one that has not yet been invented in two thousand centuries of humans fighting. Boxers didn't know how to block kicks. Manfred would be shocked as hell. He would make some stupid face like he just caught his wife cheating on him with the ripped new trainer Renato as he fell backwards on his ass, not knowing what the universe meant anymore, before sighing and closing his eyes for the last time.

"Push it... Seventeen!" barked Manfred, walking through the dark crowd. He thought he was some kind of Tyler Durden or German Joe Louis. Carlotta didn't give a damn if he was a former **GDR** amateur champion, at present he was an aging boxing instructor at a fitness studio in a strip mall.

"Jumping Jacks… *Los geht's*! One!"

Carlotta rose and flung her elbows and knees.

It smelled like fart in this tiny dungeon. It looked like it, too. Thick steam lifted steadily from the rows of sweating backs and pits and asses, mirrors collecting this floating fluid layer upon layer, nobody bothering to open a door or window, oxygen levels dropping by a percentage point with each gasp, squeal, sucking of air.

Grab ass. Carlotta could still remember his face. That face was the entire reason she chose, paid money, to put herself in this horrendous setting. What excuse the others had, she did not know.

The face of the man was what haunted her. Yes, *haunted* was a dramatic word to use, but it did, for weeks, until she convinced her coworker Darcy to join the Boom Town Boxing Club evening class with her. But Darcy the cheapskate gave up after the third class, the last free one, and now Carlotta was on her own. So be it.

"What are you doing?!" Manfred stopped and got in Carlotta's face. "Arms extended, all the way!"

Was he going to pick on her again today? Manfred was just a sad bastard who enjoyed torturing others in the safety of his domain. When did his tough guy routine get old? Carlotta clenched her teeth and stretched her arms and legs as far as they could go, swung her limbs like mighty anchors, forming a perfect circle, the *Vitruvian Woman*, Leonardo da Vinci.

The man was a regular one, good-looking even, bushy brown brows and a friendly nose like Jim from *The Office*, a black hooded sweatshirt that on another young man might have been cause for concern in this day and age. But the man walked toward the parking lot after the concert that night unremarkable and unseen, before he reached forward and grabbed Carlotta's ass—hard and long and deep and sexually—and Carlotta turned and saw his face with clarity before he ran away, escaping behind many frosty car windshields.

"Jump rope! *Move!*" Manfred went to reset the clock as everyone hurried for a good pair.

Every girl had had her ass grabbed. Carlotta knew that. But why was that supposed to change anything? Maybe, she worried as she went with the others toward the jump rope bin, a pervert was staring at her ass in tights now, thinking about how he could get away with a quick handful, a firm little squeeze. Was it worse to be a girl whose ass no one wanted to grab? It was settled, thought Carlotta. She would put on a black hooded sweatshirt tonight and go around grabbing dicks in public places. Sure, some guys might be okay with that, but if she could convince all women around the world, perhaps through a clever hashtag, to start groping men collectively, targeting them as soon as

puberty hit, all the time but especially during the hot summer months, maybe, after years and years and generations
and generations, men would come to understand ass grabbing like women do.

Carlotta found a good rope and rushed back to her spot.

Pitter-patter, pitter-patter. Heel to toe, flat then arched,
bend then straight. Her rhythm was right today. Carlotta
saw herself in the mirror, in a clear streak made from the
ceiling fan water drippings. Her face was red. Red as hell.
She looked scared and vulnerable and weak when her face
was so red. She closed her eyes and kept jumping.

She always envied the strength of others. Her
ex-boyfriend Nathaniel had a proper body. He was broad
and tall and naturally built for anything a human could need
to do on this planet. And yet with a body so powerful he did
very little with it. Even that time at the bar when a drunk
Raiders fan slapped a beer out of his hands, Nathaniel
didn't retaliate. Carlotta never knew if she admired that
about him or resented it.

One thing was clear, she would never be as strong
as him. She would never be as strong as most men. You
were stuck with what you were given in life. For most, it
was decided at birth what would be passed down to you
from previous generations. Face, body, disease, money,
property, name. Carlotta never knew her grandparents
but she knew she would always be small, never be
wealthy or powerful. She would always be an underdog

in this dangerous and unforgiving world.

Carlotta tripped over her rope. She needed water.

"Time up! Hand wraps! Gloves!" shouted Manfred.

Carlotta went to her gym bag. She forgot her water bottle. She put on her stretchy hand wraps with haste and got her blue Everlast ten-ounce boxing gloves and popped in her clear mouthguard and returned to the center of the gym, where everyone was watching Manfred. She was still out of breath when she rejoined the crowd.

For three months now Carlotta had been coming to Boom Town. On days like today, she got depressed about her slow progress. Sure she could jump rope, but was she any stronger or better at throwing a punch?

Manfred called up his favorite student Lupe to demonstrate the first drill. Lupe the Olympian freak could twist her torso like some futuristic woodchopper, jab like some futuristic piston, dip and roll and slip like some futuristic jack-in-the-box. Carlotta would never be able to box like that.

But what the hell would Carlotta do even if she could? What was she expecting to accomplish with this training? She didn't know. She hadn't thought that far ahead. Joining this class was reflex. Would she turn around and knock out anyone that ever touched her? Start busting heads in the street like some violent nut? Even if she was the best boxer in the world, so fucking what? Well, thought Carlotta, the what was that maybe she wouldn't feel so helpless and maybe this idiotic class could work even if her stance was goofy and her hook always rotated in the wrong direction.

"—Two one! Left jab, right cross, left hook!"

Damn it, Carlotta missed the first part. Her mind wandered when she was exhausted and about to puke. She would have to watch the others.

The clock beeped. Carlotta got the lumpy brown heavy bag near the dumbbell rack. Her partner on the bag was the twig kid who showed up every class, Gilbert or something. He looked fragile but had snap in his punch and sincerity in his eyes. Carlotta observed his movements.

The man had brown eyes. Or were they green? What did the man do after he ran away that night, Carlotta wondered often. Go jerk off behind a sycamore tree thinking about her ass? Or did he go assault another girl? His hair was thin and shiny and swept across his forehead. Did he have a receding hairline? She didn't think so, he was young, under thirty. Bad teeth? She thought she remembered a chip or crooked something. If she saw him again, she would recognize him. Definitely. She was pretty sure.

Carlotta hit the bag. Jab cross hook. Her punches had no snap. The sound was not of a leather whip like the kid but of someone sitting down comfortably in their favorite leather chair. Carlotta tried but could never muster real strength. If she had a core it certainly never engaged. If she had fast twitch muscles they never seemed to be activated.

The clock beeped. Carlotta gasped and wiped away

fresh snot.

"Now my darlings, left jab, right cross, left hook, *roll*, left hook, right cross, left hook. *Los geht's!*" Manfred only demonstrated combos once. He liked being able to correct everyone.

Gilbert the Kid went first. Snap snap snap. Carlotta admired him. The poor kid was probably bullied like hell in school but at least had the balls and brains to join a boxing class in his teens, not thirties.

Carlotta's turn. Left right left roll left right left. If she saw the man again, she could knock him out. A single pop to the chin. Bam. But first she would make him apologize. She would record his apology on her phone as he cried shamefully, then she would share it all over the internet.

As she thought about this, Carlotta came out of her roll with surprising momentum. Her hips twisted naturally and she grunted effortlessly and she involuntarily released a crisp, swift punch. Her first snap. It was loud.

The clock beeped. An overweight mom the next bag over glanced at Carlotta who turned, seething. That's right, bitch.

"Partner drills! Body jabs only. One at a time, offense defense, switch! Ready?! Clear?! *Los geht's!*" Manfred always got louder as the end of class got nearer.

Carlotta began lightly jabbing as the kid slipped and ducked with awkward grace.

Manfred appeared from out of the floorboards and got

in Carlotta's ear. "What is that?! Extend the jab, retract it. Quick out. Quick in. *Hit* him! *Protect* yourself!" Manfred's breath stunk. Carlotta at least had the decency to brush her teeth before class. She bit down harder into her mouthguard, exhaling spit with carbon dioxide, began jabbing like a mad woman, an overworked engine in the hull of the Titanic, burning through hot coal over the Atlantic.

"Switch!"

The kid jabbed. It terrified Carlotta. Unlike hers, his left fist came up through and between her gloves, all the time, reaching her face at will. It was shocking, disturbing. What was he doing? They were only supposed to be doing body jabs! The kid must have seen the terror in her eyes because after a few taps he eased off.

God, why was Carlotta such a pussy! Why did a person attacking her make her want to shrink and run away instead of fight back? Why did someone grabbing her ass make her brood and withdraw from society for weeks and then join a lame boxing class like that was some bold course of action?

People could sense that she was a pussy from a mile away. And they did, all her life. Like in elementary school when Joey Eash used to yell, "*Carlotta! Carlotta! Let me park my bus in your Carlotta!*" And she would just ignore him or think mean thoughts rather than crack his skull with a rock. In the office, colleagues took credit for her work all the time. And that night at the concert, even from behind, in the dark, the man in the hooded sweatshirt could recognize that there was an ass he could grab without consequence, without fight.

"Back to bags! Last two rounds, non-stop. Fire! Go!" Manfred clapped his big mitts and laughed.

Thank God. The kid was happy to punch at normal speeds again and Carlotta was glad the partner drill was over. She was angry. She was shaking. She didn't want to do that again. She had no defense, fine, but maybe she could still develop an offense. The bag work was where she could excel and be great.

Carlotta went. Only her punches were not snapping. They had regressed to their old disgraceful ways. The sweat began rolling down her forehead, stinging her eyes, as she tried to focus on the heavily duct-taped middle part of the bag, tried to imagine a face there. Perhaps the man's.

Beep. Gilbert the Kid switched in, snapping away again. Snap snap snap. The skinny little twerp. He was really starting to annoy her.

"Last round! Non-stop! Final ninety seconds! *Fire!*" This last flurry was Manfred's favorite part. Manfred and his dumb buzz cut. He might have still looked tough but he most likely wasn't. His glory days were long behind him. This wasn't his world anymore, after all.

It was Carlotta's.

Carlotta snarled and went into attack mode. Her heart rate was up and she exhaled only in short bursts. Her arms dragged and felt dense but she kept punching, as rapidly as she could. She punched and punched like someone was depending on her, like a little orphan was trapped in this heavy bag and Carlotta was the only one who could punch her way through to rescue him.

Carlotta kept punching and punching when, with thirty seconds left, something in her body arrangement, something in her movements, came together. It all suddenly made sense, like an ancient puzzle, and the punches turned loud, her punches became powerful. They snapped. They really did.

Carlota went faster, wide-eyed and smiling through her mouthguard, each furious fist bouncing off the leather like a hammer off hot steel. The balls of her feet sunk into the floorboards as her chin stayed low and her eyes focused on her target.

The clock finally beeped for the last time that evening.

"Okay! Gloves off! Time to stretch!" Manfred went to turn off the clock.

But Carlotta didn't hear the clock or Manfred as she kept punching, beautifully and cleanly. Soon the crisp snaps of her punches were the only sounds heard in the gym. The other students turned and noticed and started to come closer to see what was going on. Left right left, left right left. She had never felt so strong.

Snap snap snap.

Snap snap snap.

Snap snap, crack.

Carlotta dropped her left hand. She squealed. It was high-pitched but she didn't sound like a little girl or princess. It was a war cry. Yes, that's what it was. Carlotta punched again. There was more pain in her hand. Another war cry could be heard. She punched again, then she punched harder, then she pulled back once more to punch as hard as she had ever punched anything in her life.

But Manfred had already smashed through the crowd and was tackling the bag, launching it far back into the air, hollering, "Stop! Stop! *Stop*! No *more*!"

The bag swung back down into Manfred's spine, resting between his shoulder blades, and he grabbed Carlotta by the shoulders and shook her, looking for answers in her eyes. "What are you *doing*?"

Carlotta just stared back, huffing and trembling, at this old dog, this poor beaten man trying to give something back to a world that had long forgotten him. Her left hand hung by her hip, concealed by the puffy little synthetic leather glove.

Manfred did not know what to do. He appeared lost and guilty and worried, a look Carlotta and the other students had never seen before, and Carlotta thought for a split second about punching him in his face for some reason, but instead she fell forward into his broken body and held on, rested her face in his cheap, dirty sweatshirt. She wanted to cry. She wanted to cry so damn bad. The bones in her hand were on fire and Carlotta wanted to scream and curse and move mountains, or at least let her tears run freely, but she didn't. She only held on and continued to breathe in and out and she knew then that she was glad she joined the class. She knew she would come back to Boom Town once her hand healed, and as the music faded out and the whispers around her grew louder, Carlotta eased off the mouthguard and lifted her head momentarily and wondered only if she should take a cab or walk to the hospital which was no more than a few blocks away.

AMBROSIA

E at the stuff. Please, I beg you. I can't do it alone. The corn relish is gone. The spring rolls are dwindling. The potato salad is a spoonful away. Even the biscuits, the dry biscuits, are down to the last two. In the middle of the table sits the uneaten ambrosia, cubes of strange fruit drowning slow deaths in white glob, wincing under the summer sun. A flower-shaped bowl of disappointment, a sweating glass vessel of unfulfilled promise. How embarrassing. How painfully and unescapably embarrassing. This will crush Sam. Please, not now. Not today.

I seem to be the only one aware. So I eat and eat. But my three servings have barely put a dent in the bowl and the glob level remains high. Our friends. How can these be our friends? They are selfish and false. They do not care about Sam.

I watch Sam glance at the ambrosia here and there

throughout the barbecue, not saying a word, not even taking a spoon herself. She smiles at Priya's eager jokes, picks at pieces of burnt chicken, but her mind is elsewhere. I stop eating the other food, even the meat, and focus on the ambrosia. How can this be salad. Who decided that any cold dish involving fruit or vegetables must be called salad.

I think about what Dr. Savage said. I think about Sam's test results next week. I ask myself why I talked her into coming today.

A sports car vrooms by outside. Barry turns his head alertly, as if to suggest to everyone he has some special knowledge or interest in cars, which he doesn't. I suddenly hate Barry and his adorable girlfriend, Sophie, who brought the sweet corn relish. She probably got the recipe from some Jamie Oliver cookbook or perhaps his YouTube channel. I hate Jamie Oliver.

Sam worried ambrosia was tacky. Old-fashioned. But we didn't have much time and we already had whipped cream and sour cream sitting in the fridge, cans of Dole in the pantry. I convinced her it was a classic. A dish that knows its history and is self-aware, a salad that winks at you. I told her it was even in *Edward Scissorhands*. She couldn't remember.

Karla starts talking incessantly about her new job. Nobody cares. Certainly not me. Or Sam. Media buying or something, streaming mobile video smart content, I think, *really cool stuff nobody out there is doing, man*. Why doesn't she ask anyone else about their jobs or lives. The woman only cares about herself.

The coals are turning cold. Nothing more will go on the grill. Sebastian casually brought black forest cake. Who the hell brings homemade black forest cake to a barbecue. Everyone is ready for dessert. Ambrosia can be a side dish or a dessert. I once saw a man eat ambrosia with crackers for lunch, I had told Sam earlier. This is bad. Once we cross over into dessert, once that black forest cake comes out, the ambrosia does not stand a chance.

I can't take it anymore. It's not fair. It's mean. It hurts me to see the ambrosia sitting there shamefully, like a dancer at a strip club who nobody wants to buy a dance from yet must still walk around all night asking.

"In Greek mythology," I say loudly, "ambrosia was the food of the gods."

"I haven't had it in years," says Priya. "My aunt used to make it every summer. Those were fun visits. Oh damn, I think I must try some now."

"Reminds me of my childhood, too," says Barry. "Trips to Raging Waters, strawberry soda, dishing out wedgies."

He lines up behind Priya. There is a line for the ambrosia. I look at Sam, who also watches.

"It tastes different than I remember," says Sophie. "Nice, but more sour than sweet, really."

"I never had the stuff," says Karla's new boyfriend, Koichi, I think.

"Can I offer you some?" I plop a generous helping down onto his plate, then a fourth serving onto my own. I pass the bowl around. It gets passed around. The tiny mandarin orange slices, the little maraschino cherries, the bloated marshmallows, get passed around.

Everybody at the barbecue is eating the ambrosia.

I smile at Sam who winks back. I feel satisfied and relieved. Set free. I want to talk to my friends. Our friends. I want to tell them that the doctor found a growth in Sam's brain. I want to tell them that it could be nothing but it might be something. I want to ask why it takes five damn days to get a test result back. I want one of them to tell us everything will be okay.

The sun begins to cool. Barry puts on music, something fun. He was a pretty good DJ in college. The basketball game is on in the background. It's a close one. Sam and the girls start dancing silly in the living room. I see Sebastian think about taking out his black forest cake once or twice but he never does. He's too busy making us laugh. He could always tell a great joke.

Between songs, there's a gurgle. What was that. I listen. There are no babies or pets here. The door is closed, there are no frogs or toads. Again, even louder, we hear another gurgle. A stomach. It's coming from a human stomach.

Like a round of musical chairs has ended, Sophie makes a break for it, toward the bathroom, her pants unbuttoning before the door can slam fully closed. "Don't come in!"

"Uh-oh," says Priya. "I don't feel good."

"What's wrong?" asks Sam, concerned.

Priya rushes off in a similar direction, bent over like a small forward fouled in the paint. "I think I'm going to be sick."

"Upstairs," instructs Barry. "If you have to do something, upstairs!"

Priya leaps up the creaky wooden steps.

"Now that you mention it," says Koichi, pale in the face.

"Baby, you look awful!" says Karla.

"*Shit*," says Koichi. "This is going to get ugly."

"Well, hold it!" says Barry. "I'm out of bathrooms—"

"My house," says Sebastian confidently. "I've got three toilets at my house. Just down the street. We can make it if we hurry." He heads out the front door and down the porch steps, Karla and Koichi plus two more guests, friends of Sophie's, running closely, awkwardly behind. "Look, there! I think I see a porta-potty in the park," somebody shouts on the way out.

Barry appears from the kitchen. "Sophie, honey, there's a glass of water for you here." He then rushes past us, out the back door, a hand pressed against the bottom half of his abdomen. "Maybe the neighbors are home! Somebody must be home!" The door swings shut.

Sam and I are left alone in the living room. The house is now quiet, except for muffled sounds coming from behind closed doors, two to be exact, one upstairs and one down the hall. Sam and I listen, anonymously. Two boisterous rooms in an otherwise shy and reserved home.

Sam turns and looks at the bowl of ambrosia, nearly empty.

"How long was that cream in the fridge?" asks Sam.

"Maybe it was the sweet corn relish."

"I told you we never should have made ambrosia."

"We should leave," I say. "I'll get the bowl."

Sam and I gather our belongings and exit the barbecue, unseen by the sick or their caretakers.

The drive home is silent. We go the long way to avoid Sebastian's house. Our friends will surely hate us after this. Will they know with certainty it was the ambrosia? What if they can't go to work because of this? What if there is damage to clothing or carpet?

"We can call everyone later," I assure Sam. "Tell them we got sick too and had to leave." In truth, it's only a matter of time for me.

As we turn out of the neighborhood, Sam still does not speak. I'm not sure what to say either. I think the ambrosia tasted good. I think we were decent for making something ourselves and not buying a bag of kettle chips or making some papaya salad from a YouTube video. I think we were courageous for coming today.

But I can feel Sam's eyes narrowing. Her palms tightening around the wheel. Her breathing slowing. Please, let this pass. Let this afternoon fade away like one of those clouds on the horizon. I leave the radio off. Perhaps the accelerating summer air, the sound of other cars leaving other barbecues, will help blow everything over.

Then Sam laughs. Just a giggle. I turn. She lets another one slip. I stare at her. I stay solemn and repentant as I try to understand what Sam is doing. Then we unravel. It starts with small heaves and snorts then grows into louder, longer, larger hysteria. Sam lets out a terrible shrill. I grunt at one point. We turn red in the cheeks and fight for air. We try to focus on the lanes and stay on the road. We howl and keep howling, wickedly, spitefully, cruelly, at our friends, their suffering, their pain, the fear on Koichi's face, the urgency of Sophie's sprint, the confusion in Barry's eyes. The laughter is overwhelming. It seems to come from somewhere below, beneath the stomach, past the pancreas, lower than where the ambrosia must be sitting.

I can't remember the last time Sam and I laughed like this.

We catch the green and get on the freeway, the same one we'll take to Doctor Savage on Tuesday. Just a couple more days. Flushed and teary-eyed, Sam turns on our headlights and crosses over two lanes. She gets the car into fifth then lets off the clutch.

She places her hand in mine. I hold it tightly.

"It's fine," says Sam. "Everything's going to be okay."

SQUIRRELS

Those poor old Sutherby Squirrels. They say that. We play the Chipman Chipmunks today. The last game of this awful season. Those Chips are undefeated, you know, going to the playoffs. We, the Squirrels, are defeated I guess. Going home after today. We got an okay squad though, nothing to hang our heads about. Played some good games. Even almost won a few.

About these Squirrels, we're all Asian kids. By chance, you know. Somewhere else in America, it might seem strange that a city parks and recreation team ended up with a roster full of Asian kids, but that's what makes the Bay Area special. Some people say that. The Chipman Chipmunks, who play ten minutes away, are all Black kids, so maybe there is something to be said. Hell, in this town we got an all Mexican team. And an all White team. But it's not segregated or something like that, over at Krusi Park, on the west end, they got a team full of mixed kids. White and Guatemalan, Filipino and Black, they got a Navajo and Eskimo kid. I swear, man.

Now when I say all Asian, I mean starting five plus the bench. And specifically, the Chinese kind of Asian. If the city could afford to put last names on shirts, our team would save on letters. We got a Chen, Chan, Chung, Chin and Cho. I'm serious, no joke. There's Steve Chen, Kevin Chan, Eric Chung, Mike Chin and Jason Cho. Our middle school yearbook has five pages of "*Ch*." The Black kids on Chipman have great last names like Washington, James, Banks and, well, Chipman. Hell, they got a player named Hardaway. No fooling around. Hardaway. Unbelievable.

Anyway, we get down early, something like forty points by the half. Not our worst showing. The Squirrels wear yellow shirts, the Chipmunks wear black shirts. You can't make this stuff up. Their best player is Dontrell Wilson, a six-four thirteen-year old with a mustache. We got one good player, Jason Cho. He's a big chubby bastard, will go on next year to play high school ball. But Dontrell Wilson will go on to play pro.

And he does. Dontrell Wilson plays small forward for the Milwaukee Bucks for three seasons.

The game is not unlike past performances. Coach says we play triangle offense but I don't believe him. Me, I'm okay. I got a jump shot. I can dribble, you know, but I'm small. You can be small and good at basketball, don't get me wrong, but you better be *good* good.

Dontrell, he's got a triple-double already. And a dunk. Over poor near-sighted Kevin Chan. It's okay. We execute a couple pick-and-rolls. I mean, nobody beats a team like Chipman off fast breaks. I don't have any points yet, but hey, I got an assist. To Jason Cho that hippo. He can bang in the paint with the best of them.

The score is 71 to 14 going into the fourth.

None of the parent Squirrels came today. Chipman is not really on the good side of town. So we all said the game was cancelled and rode our bikes straight after school. But there are plenty of Chipman parents and family members watching from the stands. Sometimes they even laugh. Hell, who can blame them? Not me.

So look, with minutes left in the game, we got a few goals on our mind, none of which involve winning. One, don't get excessively embarrassed. No tomahawk jams, balls to the forehead or broken ankles. Two, don't actually break your ankles or otherwise get hurt. That's how you get the "privilege" of sports stripped from you for the remainder of school. Three, walk away from defeat chin up, a proud Squirrel. What else can you do in life? Nothing.

We bring the ball up without it getting stolen. Mike Chin passes a sloppy one to Eric Chung. Jason Cho sets a late pick. The defense doesn't bite. I jog the baseline to the deep corner. Eric bounces the ball off his butt. Regains control. Sees me. Heaves the rock cross court. Dontrell Wilson, like a gator in a zoo, watches this raw, plucked chicken sailing slow as hell over the pond. His eyes light up. He sprints toward me, toward the plunging poultry, full speed, the scent of an epic swat swirling around the air.

So get this. I catch the ball just fine. Then I throw up the best goddamn pump fake in the *history* of pump fakes. My toes damn near leave the pavement. The ball almost slips from my fingertips. And Dontrell goes soaring right *over* me, ending up damn near upside down in the bushes. Then I square up and hit just about the *prettiest* three point-er you ever saw in your life. No joke. Swish.

I backpedal arm raised, goose neck hanging. The crowd, all the Chipman family members, goes absolutely nuts. Even Dontrell's teammates hoot and grab hold of one another.

The final score is 90 to 17, Chipmunks.

The teams walk in single file for the postgame low fives. Dontrell Wilson looks me in the eye and says, "Nice shot, my man." It could have just as well been Kobe Bryant say-ing that to me. Hell of a guy, that Dontrell Wilson.

So what's the point? I don't know. But listen, fifteen years later I'm playing pickup ball in New Mexico. I'm there for work, don't ask me why. At a local YMCA near my hotel. Now, don't take this the wrong way, but in New Mexico, this part anyway, I don't think they got a whole lot of Blacks or Asians. It's a tough game. Everyone is sweaty as hell after. Then this guy from the other team comes over and says, "You're pretty good for an Asian." He says that.

"Thanks," I say, sounding sincere, too. "You know, I once sank a three pointer over Dontrell Wilson."

"*Dontrell* Wilson?"

"Dontrell Wilson."

"No kidding?"

"I swear, man."

LIKE A NORWEGIAN

*A*rrival:

"If the ship sinks, just grab hold of *that*," said Mr. Potts inside the elevator, pointing to a poster of Nelly Vasquez, the whale of a woman scheduled to sing each night after dinner service in the Moonlight Lounge. A mother near the doors glared and told her son, "Ignore the stupid idiot." Oh what, thought Mr. Potts. The lady wasn't a big blubbery beast? The elevator dinged. Mr. Potts got his bags and headed out for his cabin. This was going to be a relaxing eight-day vacation.

Day 1:

What a slogan the cruise line had! Cruise Like a Norwegian. The sail-away party had different-colored signs saying things like *Party* Like a Norwegian or *Dine* Like a Norwegian. The staff members even encouraged guests, *"There you go, Mrs. Gibbs, Hot Tubbing Like a Norwegian!"* Mr. Potts had never known a real Norwegian, but he imagined they might take offense. After all, were Norwegians a lazy and entitled people like the guests on this ship? He wanted to ask one, but there weren't any on board.

Day 2:

Every morning, the staff members greeted Mr. Potts with a big smile. Sure, that works on the old timers, thought Mr. Potts. They probably feel like real VIPs here! Most of the guests were senior citizens. The rest were families or couples. Mr. Potts seemed to be the only guest traveling alone. Not that he didn't have friends back home. He made sure any inquiring guest knew this when they asked him why he was "cruising" solo. All of his friends still *worked*, alright? None of them could spare their vacation hours. And he just happened to be single at the *moment*, okay? Of course he had had girlfriends before. Is that acceptable? Is that fine with you, he would sometimes reply, not in those exact words. These people were worse than the ones back home. Be Interrogated Like a Norwegian, thought Mr. Potts.

Day 3:

The food was terrible. But the old timers loved it. The waiters would come by and ask, *"How was everything, Mr. Henry?"* And Mr. Henry would smile and reply, *"Just perfect! Absolutely exquisite!"* Meanwhile, Mr. Potts wanted to barf. They served dishes like Salisbury Steak or Chicken

Parmesan or Asian Beef Noodles, that classic national dish of the continent of Asia. Mr. Potts would eat alone in the dining room, observing the poor old war veterans with faded forearm tattoos and military baseball caps, probably dragged on board by their wives or children. Who knew what they saw the last time they were on a ship. They just sat there with blank looks on their faces. Mr. Potts knew they recognized this place for the circus it was, like him. Eat Shitty Dinners Like a Norwegian.

Day 4:
The pool was a disgusting affair. Mr. Potts remembered the advertisements months ago of beautiful bodies poolside. Glistening legs. Firm asses. But here, everyone was obese, pale and hairy, including the women. And nobody seemed to care! The worse the body, the smaller the bathing suit. Go Blind Like a Norwegian. Sometimes, a stranger would start a conversation with Mr. Potts in the hot tub. Mr. Potts would simply close his eyes as if enjoying the bubbles too much to talk, and eventually the stranger would leave him alone. It worked every time. Mr. Potts was very satisfied with this and practiced getting even better at it. Avoid Small Talk Like a Norwegian.

Day 5:
There was a live show nightly in the Stardust Theater. It depressed Mr. Potts. If the performers were bad, he felt

embarrassed for them. If the performers were good, he wondered what went wrong in their lives that they ended up here, on this pathetic cruise ship, rather than on the radio or on Broadway. Oh, and these real sexy shows? They depressed Mr. Potts, too. He watched these pretty girls strut around stage, cleavage out, and thought the old timers must get sad knowing they couldn't get it up anymore. Or maybe they got it up just dandy, but got sad anyway seeing their wives in the same room as these bouncy young things. Marriage sure is for suckers, thought Mr. Potts as he sipped his coconut daiquiri in the dark. Enjoy the Show Like a Norwegian.

Day 6:

Games with the staff came after lunch. Mr. Potts refused to spend time with people *paid* to spend time with him. He wasn't a charity case! Mr. Potts's mother got a kick out of this stuff. She always loved cruises. But as she got older and sicker she couldn't go on them anymore. She was actually the one who recommended a cruise to Mr. Potts. She worried about her son. Mr. Potts had told her about his recent nervous breakdown at work, how he stopped talking to everyone for a whole week. Why should his company get any more freebies out of him? If they didn't give more than the bare minimum, why should he? He was this close to quitting! But Mr. Potts's mother convinced him a cruise might help clear his head. She never understood why he took his career so serious. After all, what was so important about being an account manager for the nation's third-largest window blinds company? Mr. Potts could never explain it to her right. He spent the afternoon watching the games from afar, occasionally laughing at the fools. Keep Your Distance Like a Norwegian.

Day 7:
Formal night was a big deal. Men wore jackets and women wore dresses. It was the same terrible food, now divided into four courses. Mr. Potts got his table for one. This time, they put him near the kitchen doors. Mr. Potts drank four gin martinis, one for each course. Afterwards, he felt like paying Nelly Vasquez and the Norwegian House Band a visit. Mr. Potts made his way to the Moonlight Lounge and plopped down in the front row. Whoa, *Nelly!* thought Mr. Potts. The woman could sing! Mr. Potts drank and drank and watched that big ass of Nelly Vasquez bounce back and forth on stage, flexing the floorboards. During her last song, Nelly Vasquez even winked at Mr. Potts. He blew a big wet floating kiss back at her. Then he passed out in his lounge chair. Get Piss Drunk Like a Norwegian. He was finally getting the hang of this.

Day 8:
Mr. Potts was hung over. But that's not why he spent most of the last sea day in his cabin. He had this awful habit

of spending the ends of his vacations planning his re-entry into society. He thought about what he had to do at work on Monday, about the several apology emails he wanted to write, about visiting his mother in the hospital and telling her how great the cruise was. She would like that. Mr. Potts then walked around the deck. He ate dinner in the less-crowded twenty-four-hour cafeteria. He gambled at the casino and lost forty dollars. He drank a pint of beer at the Irish pub. Then he went back to the Moonlight Lounge. Nelly Vasquez was already singing. Mr. Potts sat in the front row again. After a few songs, Nelly started with a slow version of *The Love Boat* theme song. Hah! thought Mr. Potts. *The Love Boat theme song*, for Christ's sake! God, he always hated that show.

> *… Love, exciting and new*
> *Come aboard. We're expecting you.*
> *And Love, life's sweetest reward.*
> *Let it flow, it floats back to you.*

Mr. Potts glanced around to see if anyone else was as embarrassed as him. This was really a stupid song!

> *… And Love won't hurt anymore*
> *It's an open smile on a friendly shore.*
> *Yes, LOOOOOOOOOOOOOOOOVE!*

Then Mr. Potts started to cry. Tears and all. He couldn't stop. He cried and continued to cry, sitting there alone in the front row of the Moonlight Lounge on Deck Seven of the Norwegian Pearl, listening to The Love Boat theme song. The tears flowed and Mr. Potts, trembly and wet, didn't know why or how to stop them. Nobody came with a tissue or asked if he was okay. Mr. Potts just sat there, a quiet mess. Finally the song ended and eventually Mr. Potts pulled himself together. After the band left and he had ordered another drink, he wondered more about the crying, specifically if anyone saw it. He didn't think so. Perhaps just Nelly Vasquez. Oh, what did he care. She probably cried every time the buffet ran out of riblets! Mr. Potts paid his tab and got up to go to his cabin. A pointless end to a pointless vacation. Well, thought Mr. Potts, at least it was almost over.

Mr. Potts dried his eyes once more in the elevator. He pressed the button. After one deck, the car stopped and the doors opened. "Well, if it isn't the lone sailor himself. I must say, sweetheart, I think you and me are the only two lookers on this whole God-*awful* boat." Mr. Potts looked up. It was Nelly Vasquez, wink and all. He sniffled. Then, without a word, he reached forward and put his arms around that big fantastic body of hers and pulled it right up against his. He kissed her. Nelly Vasquez had had groupies before, so she was startled but not shocked as she kissed the poor chap back. Mr. Potts held on tight and didn't let go. She smelled sweet. She was warm and soft and round and the only thing in this world he ever wanted. The elevator dinged and two people got out. Mr. Potts could pack in the morning. Make Love Like a Norwegian.

RECENT CONVERSATIONS

Tell me the secret Jane
March 6

Secret what secret
Jane March 7

To happiness
March 7

Love?
Jane March 7

I love my cat
March 7

She doesn't love you back
Jane March 7

He does I choose to believe
March 7

Cats are easier to lure into love than humans, even if sure
they are withdrawn and emotionally distant
Jane March 7

I didn't lure him and many things are easier for animals,
that's why they don't need an app
March 7

Agreed, humans and cats are different
Jane March 8

Can you find happiness without love?
March 8

I've done it successfully most of my adult life
Jane March 8

You don't like relationships?
March 8

I also don't like music and food
Jane March 8

Stupid question
March 8

Tell me the secret, is that your opener for every girl?
Jane March 8

I don't have a better one yet
March 8

I want to cover your body in green paint and spank you
like an unripe avocado
Jane March 8

Do you like spanking?
March 8

You're a serial monogamist I can tell
Jane March 8

Or to be spanked
March 8

There's a sense of desperation in your messages
Jane March 8

My mother always said those who live in a glass house...
March 8

I'm wrong?
Jane March 8

I just got out of a long relationship recently, you're right
March 8

Why did it end?
Jane March 8

The truth?
March 8

Tell me lies, tell me sweet little lies…
Jane March 8

People change. You grow together, apart, life's filters change. One day you wake up and look at each other and it's different
March 8

All relationships have to end I guess, either by falling out of love or death eventually
Jane March 8

That's one way to look at it
March 8

You find it depressing?
Jane March 8

I think it can be beautiful, what's the alternative live and die
alone with your cats?
March 8

You like to share
Jane March 8

It's easier to say things to a stranger, anyway we may never
meet in person
March 8

As most of these conversations go
Jane March 8

But I hope not
March 8

Because you like how I look in my pictures?
Jane March 8

You have a sad smile
March 8

LIKE A CHAMPION

My mother used to tell me that every night before bed
Jane March 8

Do you have work tomorrow?
March 8

What's work?
Jane March 8

Good morning sorry I fell asleep
March 9

Please don't say that we don't even know each other
Jane March 9

What's on the agenda today Jane?
March 9

Plotting world domination
Jane March 9

Any progress?
March 9

And learning Maya
Jane March 9

You speak a second language?
March 9

Animation software
Jane March 9

You're smart
March 9

Oh no, you're not…
Jane March 9

You're a designer?
March 9

I'm my own boss, great isn't it?
Jane March 9

I work in a cubicle
March 9

That explains it
Jane March 9

Without a cool job, I'm forced to find fulfillment in other places
March 9

Swingers clubs?
Jane March 9

Kayaking, salsa dancing, beat making, trying new food, other hobbies
March 9

Those are certainly hobbies
Jane March 9

Do you like to go to swingers clubs?
March 9

You should know I'm vegetarian
Jane March 9

What should I know
March 9

If trying new food is important to you, dating a vegetarian might be hard as much of trying new food is heavy on the meat
Jane March 9

So you only date other vegetarians?
March 9

> I have
> *Jane March 9*

If I play tennis should I only date other tennis players?
March 9

> Ask Andre Agassi and Steffi Graf
> *Jane March 9*

They might say opposites attract
March 9

> What do you say
> *Jane March 9*

I think superficial things like what you eat or what you do
for exercise have little to do with who you are
March 9

> Relationships are hard enough why add the extra strain of
> fighting over jazz or techno every night
> *Jane March 9*

I'm glad you're considering the idea of us eating food together
March 9

That was unintentional
Jane March 9

How about this weekend?
March 9

This weekend what
Jane March 9

Friday night, want to have dinner together?
March 9

You want to have dinner together?
Jane March 9

We seem to have lots to talk about
March 9

Because we're opposites?
Jane March 9

Could be fun, I think we'd have fun
March 9

Let me check and get back to you later, is that okay?
Jane March 9

Sure just let me know
March 9

                              Sorry, how was your weekend?
                                   Jane March 14

Okay fine, yours was busy?
March 14

   Were you able to find another date to go to dinner with?
                                   Jane March 14

My cat, we went Dutch
March 14

                                   That's sweet
                                   Jane March 14

Should we still reschedule?
March 14

          Yes sorry it's just a bad time, having a bad week
                                   Jane March 14

Everything okay?
March 14

People are the worst
Jane March 14

Best to avoid them sometimes
March 14

Maybe some of us just naturally share a stronger cosmic
bond, others never stand a chance
Jane March 14

I wouldn't disagree
March 14

Extrapolate that and ask, do soul mates exist?
Jane March 14

If every person you ever loved stood in a room, you would
probably gravitate toward one
March 14

That's a soul mate?
Jane March 14

Finding 1 human out of 6 billion that you want to share life
with, not the worst definition
March 14

Have you been out in the city when the weather's nice? There are beautiful people everywhere, ones you're sexually attracted to, many are even kindhearted
Jane March 14

We're all interchangeable then?
March 14

*7 billion
Jane March 14

Maybe the answer lies in swingers clubs then
March 14

Interchangeable only to a point I admit, we're all uniquely broken when you get close, it's about when and how you discover the broken parts
Jane March 14

It's about finding someone with compatible broken parts
March 14

That's funny, I like that
Jane March 14

What's broken with you?
March 14

LIKE A CHAMPION

Slow healing and forgetting gene, you?
Jane March 14

Impaired vision of the trees, only the forest
March 14

Glasses help
Jane March 14

Next week I'll see trees in Oregon for a training seminar
March 14

Sounds like a nightmare
Jane March 14

Maybe we could meet before I leave?
March 14

You sure you want that kind of excitement before a big trip?
Jane March 14

I told my friend you're probably a catfish
March 14

I'm a 60-year old man using the computers at the public
library
Jane March 14

Your proficiency with the World Wide Web is something to
be proud of
March 14

> Okay
> *Jane March 14*

Yeah?
March 14

> Wait, too late to change my mind?
> *Jane March 14*

Dinner Thursday night at eight
March 14

> Where?
> *Jane March 14*

Trust me to pick a vegetarian place?
March 14

> No
> *Jane March 14*

Perfect, this will be fun
March 14

Okay, now get back to work already you crazy person
Jane March 14

Jane I found the perfect place, Pretty Peas
March 15

Do you want to meet there or should we meet somewhere earlier?
March 17

Heading out now to Pretty Peas, just message me if you're lost or running late or anything…
March 17

Hey
Jane June 1

What
June 3

What are you doing?
Jane June 3

Working
June 3

I was thinking about you
Jane June 3

There's a flu going around I heard
June 3

I'm glad you're still on here
Jane June 3

Let me guess, you and the other guy broke up?
June 3

He was a vegetarian, was never going to work
Jane June 3

I'm very sympathetic to your pain
June 3

I'm really sorry about before, I'm bad with this stuff. I started seeing him and it felt unfair to keep messaging you
Jane 6 hours ago

You could have said that
4 hours ago

Bad dating app etiquette, I know
Jane 4 hours ago

Seems to be a common theme I've learned the past few months
4 hours ago

That's why I'm getting off
Jane 4 hours ago

Only bars and supermarket aisles from now on?
3 hours ago

Trying to let things unfold naturally
Jane 3 hours ago

That's brave
2 hours ago

You can't plot everything in life, take a road and see where it leads
Jane 2 hours ago

Better to drive off a cliff yourself than have Google Maps drive you off it
2 hours ago

I have a crazy idea before I delete my account
Jane 2 hours ago

Print out all your embarrassing conversations and turn them into a book?
2 hours ago

No, where do you work?
Jane 2 hours ago

Near the stadium why
1 hour ago

When do you get off?
Jane 1 hour ago

Soon why
1 hour ago

I want to come see you, can we meet at the big statue?
Jane 1 hour ago

Meet today?
55 minutes ago

I'm on the way there anyway
Jane 55 minutes ago

To do what?
50 minutes ago

I didn't think that far ahead
Jane 50 minutes ago

So will you join me?
Jane 30 minutes ago

I'll probably regret this but fine, leaving the office now
20 minutes ago

I'm kind of nervous for some reason
Jane 20 minutes ago

Maybe because I'm really the catfish
20 minutes ago

Now I'm curious
Jane 20 minutes ago

You mean the bronze statue at the main entrance?
18 minutes ago

The ugly one
Jane 17 minutes ago

Tell me, is your name really Jane?
15 minutes ago

That's what it says on my profile
Jane 15 minutes ago

Some people use fake names
15 minutes ago

Don't worry, you'll recognize me
Jane 12 minutes ago

I just looked again, you removed all your pictures
12 minutes ago

And I got a haircut recently
Jane 11 minutes ago

Great
10 minutes ago

You'll recognize me
Jane 8 minutes ago

I forgot to tell you I gained 50 pounds
6 minutes ago

Hurry up already
Jane 6 minutes ago

It's crowded
5 minutes ago

I'm here
Jane 4 minutes ago

There are a lot of people
3 minutes ago

I'm wearing a red sweater
Jane 2 minutes ago

Okay, I think I see you
Just now

OVERSEAS CLUB

Before Bernie showed up, there were plenty of people and things Beatrice hated more at the Waldo Institute. Beatrice hated how much it rained there. That had little to do with the institute itself, of course, but who could Beatrice blame? God? The big umbrella corporations? She hated the lunch cantine. They served stew, or *Eintopf*, meaning "one pot," every single day, whether it was *Weihnachtsmarkt* season or *Biergarten* weather, though to be fair, Beatrice eventually admitted, summer was pretty short and most of the year it was cold, not to mention rainy, so stew was not the worst choice but anyway it always tasted terrible. Beatrice hated the head instructor Gerry, a fat ginger Englishman who couldn't effectively teach English if his jolly life depended on it. She hated the other instructors, too. But Beatrice hated most that she had moved from Bakersfield to Bavaria to teach English at an international school for rich kids and her quality of life had not elevated with her improved, though certainly not undeserved, salary but had remained largely the same as back home, if not actually a little worse. She was still the same Beatrice on this side of the world as the other.

Her first months at the institute were bad. Upon arrival, nobody seemed to like Beatrice or her opinions, which she had always been, since a young age, encouraged to share freely and her impressive training and USA experience did not help matters. She was aggressively shun not just from the Germans but the Brits, the Irish, the Spaniards, the Koreans, the French and the Taiwanese.

There was one whole month when Beatrice brought her lunch from home and ate alone at her desk, pretending simultaneously to grade, quite enthusiastically, old tests so that if someone walked by her classroom door and peeked in they wouldn't think she was some kind of totally pathetic loner or loser but rather a passionate educator who went the extra mile, or kilometer, and simply did not have time to join the others in the cantine or even eat comfortably with two free hands for that matter. By the end of that month, Beatrice missed Eintopf.

But Beatrice came up with a strategy. She read in an article online about the importance of having a workplace persona, a set of easily identifiable characteristics separate from daily tasks that would enable others to more quickly connect with you on a personal level. For instance, everyone knew that Janty liked to drink wine, probably by the jug, and that Dirk performed magic shows on the weekends, most likely for free.

Beatrice had more to work with than that. She was the only American. She drank tea, not coffee. She wore charismatic socks. She knew movies pretty well and often caught new ones the week they came out in the nearby "original language" cinema. Beatrice began promoting these little things about herself, bringing them to the forefront of her chit chats and small talk, and it worked. Soon, colleagues began making playful American "bashing" jokes and leaving the water kettle out for her in the kitchen and commenting about her absolutely wild pink and green polka-dot socks and asking her if anything good from Hollywood was currently playing.

It was wonderful, that week. Beatrice hadn't felt such a strong sense of who she was since, well, maybe ever. Back home, she was just another girl from a lower-middle-class family who wasn't exotic or especially pretty and did okay in school and okay in some sports and might have had a strong opinion about things, especially those having to deal with political or social or religious or gender or animal injustices, and a tendency to overshare these opinions, but most people didn't terribly like or dislike this about her, they mostly didn't pay that much attention.

The real haters came when Beatrice got her overseas job in *Europe*. At least that's what Beatrice guessed from the attendance at her farewell fondue party.

But all that was in the past, Beatrice began to think. She had found her new home in Germany. She could really be herself at this place. Here, Beatrice could be *Beatrice*.

Then Bernie showed up.

Bernie looked how Beatrice imagined foreigners imagined Americans looked. She was blonde, tanned and had bright white teeth. She was from Dallas and even had a Texas accent, which sounded more American than Beatrice's Central Valley, daughter-of-immigrants accent. Bernie even had a better name. It was kind of like Beatrice but zingier. Ber-n*ie*. Bernie not only drank tea but had her own handmade teapot. She not only wore charismatic socks but charismatic shoes to match. And she not only knew movies but once worked at a movie theater before deciding to become a teacher. She was also better looking. Bernie must have been thirty or thirty-five but still had a great figure and the ass of a fifteen-year-old. That seemed inappropriate to think, Beatrice recognized, but it was true. Though did fifteen-year-olds have nice asses? Their asses were probably a little underdeveloped and Bernie's ass was not underdeveloped but firm and healthy, not that Beatrice spent time thinking about Bernie's ass or fifteen-year-olds' asses, certainly not.

The worst part about Bernie's arrival though was not her butt or name or hometown, it was that Bernie didn't seem to want to be friends with Beatrice even though they were the only Americans—American women at that.

It was a fall morning on the *U-Bahn* train when Beatrice saw Bernie sitting alone and sat across from her. Bernie was reading a book. She didn't look up so Beatrice began to speak.

"So how do you like Waldo so far?" whispered Beatrice. "When exactly did you arrive? Did you get any bad apples in your class? The French kids are the *worst*. Have you gotten used to Germany yet? The mustard comes in *tubes*! Nobody jaywalks. Everything is *closed* on Sundays. They call cell phones *Handys*! Don't get me started on the language, Bernie. Do you speak German yet?"

"Well, hello to you, too!" said Bernie. She smiled above her book cover, *Der Zauberberg*. "My grandmother was German so I learned some from her, plus I took German all through high school and spent two years in Berlin after college."

"Oh," said Beatrice.

"Where are you from?" asked Bernie.

"Same place as you." Beatrice frowned. "Can't you tell?"

"Texas?"

"Bakersfield. I meant same place as you because I'm from the U.S., or States, or America, however they call it these days. I've never been to Texas, though I imagine it's a bit like Bakersfield. Let me guess, a lot of dust and cows and cow shit and not much culture? Not like here in Europe anyway."

"Oh, I miss Dallas already."

"Me, *too*. Bakersfield, I mean. I had a great life there before I came here. I didn't come to escape or anything like that."

"Of course not."

"Not that I was thinking that about you," said Beatrice.

"I sure hope not!" Bernie smiled politely then went ahead and put away her book.

"So what do you hate most about living here so far?"

"Hate? Actually, I like it. Very much. You don't?"

"Well, I don't like the people sometimes, and the weather stinks. Everyone stares and it's too clean, and the food isn't the greatest but the service is bad anyway. The cars are small and everyone is too healthy. I miss having obese people around, in comparison I feel like a fat old slab of—"

"I forgot! I need to pick up potato salad for the pot-luck!" Bernie looked at the train monitor and grabbed her tote bag.

"Potluck?" asked Beatrice.

"Shoot, I'm going to be late," said Bernie. "It was nice meeting you, I've heard your name around campus."

"Beatrice. There's only one."

"See you around." Bernie hurried toward the closing doors and did a little ballet jump through them. The Aldi supermarket was just down the street from the station.

"Don't forget to bring *cash*!" shouted Beatrice. "They don't take credit cards! And don't buy the frozen lasagna, they found *horse* meat in it last summer!"

That went well, thought Beatrice.

Later that day at lunch, Beatrice went to the faculty breakroom with a plastic container full of leftover chicken breast. She really had made too much chicken the previous night and wouldn't be able to join the others in the cantine on this particular day. But when Beatrice opened the door to the breakroom, everyone was there.

The tables were joined together and all the usual ambassadors were present. The Germans, the Brits, the Irish, the Spaniards, the Koreans, the French, the Taiwanese and, lo and behold… the Americans. Bernie was sitting at the head.

"Whoa, quite a *feast*, you guys! Don't over do it, German engineering only applies to cars, not the *plumbing*!" said Beatrice.

A few of the people hummed and smiled graciously then they returned to their conversation. It involved some funny story about the airport and security check and sit not zit, from what Beatrice could gather. She warmed up her chicken in the microwave then quietly found a fork and knife and a paper towel, moving more slowly than usual, then finally left without a word and walked down the hallway and out of the brick building and through the busy grass courtyard, occasionally shouting *"Achtung!"* at the running school children, before entering *Haus 2* and walking down another hallway to get to her classroom.

She had papers to grade.

After afternoon class, Beatrice went to the small kitchen and was glad to see Hui standing patiently by the water kettle.

"Hui, what the *hell* was that earlier?" asked Beatrice.

"What the hell what?" said Hui.

"At lunch."

"The potluck?"

"*Why* was there a potluck?"

"Good question," said Hui thoughtfully. "I think Bernie came up with the idea? She calls it the Overseas Club. We get together and talk about where we're from and what we like about it here and exchange stories about our experiences in a foreign land. Neat idea, right?"

"Overseas Club? Why wasn't I invited? I saw Dirk sitting there and he's not *overseas!*"

"Interesting point. You know what? I bet Bernie probably forgot to invite you."

"*Forgot?*"

"Just come next time. We have another Overseas Club meeting on Friday at the Cuba Bar in the city center."

"*Meeting?*" Beatrice started to get flashbacks of high school student government. She was impeached as class treasurer her senior year.

"Oh relax, it's not so serious," said Hui. "Bernie is new and just wants to make friends here I think."

"Join the club!"

"Yes, that's why there's a club. The *Overseas* Club!"

"That's a terrible name."

"You have a better one?"

"Look Hui, are you going to this meeting Friday night?"

"Right, and who's going to babysit the girls. *You?*"

"I need an Earl Grey."

"The hot water's finished."

Hui handed Beatrice the empty kettle and took her full thermos with her back to her classroom. Beatrice turned on the faucet.

Beatrice didn't usually wear makeup but after work Friday, she decided to put some on. The Cuba Bar was in the city center not in redneck county like the Waldo Institute. Did they say "redneck" here? Anyway, the place sounded undoubtedly more worldly. She had never been to Cuba but then again most Americans hadn't. Had Bernie? Is that why she chose the place? Beatrice should probably brush up on her Spanish before going. Did she have any Cuban stories to tell? She did come from a state where the majority population was Latino. Though did Cubans and Mexicans, the kind of Latino popular in California, get along? Well, race relations was probably the perfect topic to discuss at a meeting of a group called the Overseas Club.

Beatrice took the U-Bahn train in the opposite direction of work and got off at the main station, the Hauptbahnhof, then walked fifteen minutes to the Cuba Bar. When she got inside there were only university kids.

"Beatrice! Over here!"

She turned and saw Emiliano and his dark curly hair, sitting alone at a table with his phone and an empty wine glass nearby.

"Meeting got cancelled," said Emiliano. "I forgot to check the Facebook group."

"What the *hell*, there's a Facebook group?" asked Beatrice.

"Well, see you Monday then."

"Should we get some mojitos anyway?" asked Beatrice. Emiliano was not the worst- looking guy on the institute's payroll, not to mention that adorable accent, and why should expensive makeup go to waste on a room full of pimply faced coeds.

"Just us two?"

"Sure."

"Well, I made plans already now to meet other friends."

"Oh."

"I would invite you but they don't speak English."

"Emiliano, when is the next Overseas Club meeting?"

"You better ask Bernie, she is *Il Presidente*." Emiliano answered his phone and waved farewell as he walked toward the door.

Beatrice thought about ordering a drink anyway but the menu was sticky and three-Euro mojitos could not be of high quality so she waited five minutes so as not to run into

Emiliano outside and then she left and walked back to the Hauptbahnhof. The city was so beautiful at night, she told herself. It was really beautiful. Damn beautiful, she kept telling herself as she stood alone in the cold and waited for her train which would come in forty-five minutes because of a fallen tree branch on the tracks.

On Monday, Beatrice went early to lunch and got her Eintopf from the cantine to go and ate in her classroom and avoided the faculty breakroom entirely. After afternoon class, Beatrice decided she wanted to go and see Bernie directly in her classroom.

Bernie was finishing up when Beatrice arrived. Beatrice opened the door a crack and watched.

"...*You might think that as an individual, there's nothing you can do to change the world, but I believe history tells us the exact opposite. That if you are someone who can tap into the spirit of the times, the zeitgeist, you can make movements where people actually move for you. This is something we see time and again in history, the right person saying something at the right time and changing the world...*"

For Pete's sake, thought Beatrice. She was even an excellent teacher. The students were engaged, listening, paying attention to each word Miss Gunner was saying. Especially some of the boys, Beatrice noticed.

The bell rang. The students scurried past Beatrice who propped the door open for them with her arm.

She walked in and applauded. "Heck of a class, Bernie!"

"Oh, history is always a hard subject," said Bernie. "It

definitely wasn't my favorite in school."

"You were terrific, really," said Beatrice. Then she whispered, "Just so you know, the tall one in front was checking out your ass while you wrote on the white board."

"Anton?" Bernie sighed, disappointed. "Boys will be boys, I guess."

"I don't think any of my students are checking out my backside!"

Beatrice laughed politely. "Nonsense, you have a great figure!"

"I used to play volleyball."

"Is there anything I can help you with, Beatrice?"

"I just came to say hello."

"Oh, that's very nice of you, how is your—"

"Actually, I did want to ask you something." Beatrice sat down on the edge of Bernie's desk and looked at her. "Why didn't you invite me to join your Overseas Club?"

Bernie turned bright red in the face. "Overseas Club? That's not an official name or anything! Gosh, it makes it sound so serious!"

"But why wasn't I invited?"

"I'm sorry, I must have simply forgotten! The concept was to have one representative from each country and I guess I figured I sort of filled the U.S. quota."

"Well, can't you make an *exception* or something?"

"Of course! Sure, why not! I just didn't know you wanted to join us, you always seemed to like doing your own thing."

"Well, you're wrong. I'd like to join."

"Okay. No problem. Great. I'll make sure you receive an invite to any and all upcoming Overseas Club activities."

"Perfect," said Beatrice.

"*Wonderful*," said Bernie.

They both continued smiling.

Then Beatrice wiggled off the desk and walked out of the classroom without another word, forgetting to close the door behind her.

Over the next three months, Beatrice did not receive any invitation from the Overseas Club. There was no email or text message or call or Facebook message or Post-It note about any meeting, potluck, bike ride or salsa night. Not from Bernie or anyone else in the Overseas Club.

It got to a point that whenever Beatrice saw a group of colleagues consisting of more than four or five people, she didn't know whether it was a spontaneous gathering or an official Overseas Club meeting, so she simply began avoiding groups altogether. She stopped going to the cantine. She stopped making an effort to talk about movies and tea and even stopped pairing her charismatic socks as strategically as she once did. She actively avoided Bernie.

Sometimes in the mornings she would see Bernie casually reading her German books on the U-Bahn train but she wouldn't sit next to her. Anyway, it's not like Bernie came and sat beside her.

It was fine, thought Beatrice. She could be a happy lone

wolf. She had been a lone wolf at different periods all her life. After all, that was part of the reason she moved to a new country. After so many years of living in the town she grew up in, having the same small circle of friends, dating the same loser guys, working at the same dead-end school with the same dispassionate teachers, she just wanted to get away from people. *Those* people. But her assumption was that she would meet new, better people that would recognize how incredible Beatrice was and everything would be great. Well, that's why you shouldn't make assumptions. She should practice what she preached to her students.

Anyway, this wasn't her first rodeo. Beatrice had been rejected by groups before. All kinds. But what was it this time? Why wasn't she worthy enough to join *this* club? Was it something about her, Beatrice, as a *person*?

Was she not American enough for Bernie? Not international enough? Not strong enough? Not feminine enough? Not a talented enough teacher? Not nice enough?

Horse shit. Any organization would be lucky to have her. She was a good person, she knew that much. And isn't that what it all boiled down to anyway? What everything in life boiled down to? Being a good person?

There was that time when she found a wallet on the seat of the transit bus with a hundred Euros in it, and what did Beatrice do? She didn't take the cash, she went to the grumpy old fellow's home and delivered it to him for barely a *Danke schön*. She could have used that money, too.

Though there was also that time in high school when some girls wanted to fight her best friend, Lizzy Riviera, and after school they had her surrounded, three of them, and Beatrice saw them by the softball dugout but was so scared, so damn scared, that she just kept walking. There was no way they would all jump Lizzy, she had reasoned, but if she had stopped to intervene, three on two was a fairer fight and something would have definitely went down. Something went down anyway and Lizzy never talked to Beatrice after that day.

But everyone made mistakes. Bernie was certainly no exception. Maybe back in Dallas, Bernie was an arsonist or kleptomaniac or serial killer. Maybe Hui sold crack in Taipei. Maybe Emiliano ripped off senior citizens in Tuscany.

Just because you walked around smiling and being friendly to everyone, that didn't make you a good person. What if you were rude and vulgar to everyone but had a heart of gold and made the right decisions in crunch time, when it truly mattered? Well, Beatrice decided, she would rather be that any day of the week. She was a good person and moving overseas, leaving her comfort zone and trying something new, was the kind of life experience that was supposed to make you a better person.

But maybe it hadn't.

By the end of spring quarter, Beatrice stopped caring.

It was petty and stupid. She knew that. Why should she let some office clique affect her emotional well-being? She was still in a beautiful country, even though she didn't speak the language, and she still had a great flat, even though it kind of smelled sometimes, and she had rewarding hobbies like yoga, even though she wasn't very good at it. Her life was complete, more or less, with or without the Overseas Club.

Beatrice just had to finish the school year strong. She wanted to make some kind of meaningful impact on her students during her time here and then evaluate the whole year objectively. She would decide then, and only then, if she wanted to renew her contract and stay in Germany.

But it was getting increasingly difficult to focus.

Beatrice really started to hate that woman.

Her hatred for Bernie eventually developed into something broader, something that snuck its way into her classroom, and before long Beatrice caught herself snapping at students and succumbing to a few ferocious outbursts that were quite unfair. Her kids were sweet. They were handling the material just fine. Beatrice hardly recognized herself when these strange flashes happened and that frustrated her more than anything.

Her decline in performance went on for weeks. So one day when the head instructor Gerry asked Beatrice to come to his office to talk privately for the first time since her arrival in the fall, Beatrice was not entirely surprised.

Gerry asked to meet on a Friday afternoon. Beatrice

had read online once that Friday was the most popular day of the week for a company to fire someone. She was nervous but prepared when she arrived a few minutes early to Gerry's office and knocked gently.

"Come on in," said Gerry.

Gerry's office had wood paneling and plants and felt respectable. There was a clear view of the mountains through the window and when Beatrice walked in she could imagine all of the beautiful old castles tucked away peacefully in the thick shadows of the green hillsides.

"Go on, have a seat Bea," said Gerry. He finished scribbling something then stood up. "Can I get you anything to drink? Tea? No, bloody hell you're an American, coffee isn't it?" He laughed.

"I'm fine," said Beatrice.

Gerry walked to the windowsill and sat uncomfortably. "How are you doing? Adjusting well to living in another country? It's tough, I can tell you. Almost a year now for you, isn't it? I really admire how well you're holding up here, Bea. It's something to be proud of."

"Thanks, Gerry."

He adjusted his cuffs and stood again. "How are your students' preparations coming for final exams? Well prepared, are they?"

"Is everything okay, Gerry?"

"Actually, I wanted to talk to you about Bernie," said Gerry.

"*Bernie?*" Beatrice furrowed her brow.

"It's come to my attention that some complaints, or rather, some rumors about Bernie are floating around campus. Nothing serious, just the beginning of the process we must do here, German bureaucracy, you know!" Gerry laughed abruptly. "I'm just conducting a few preliminary interviews in-house to get a sense of the situation before proceeding with anything so to say, more official."

"Okay."

"Beatrice, have you noticed any sort of relationships between Bernie and any of her students that might be considered inappropriate?" Gerry turned and faced the window. "With some of the older boys, for example."

"*Inappropriate?*"

"Inappropriate. Whatever the word means to you."

Of course not, thought Beatrice. She had seen Bernie in action. She was a decent, honest, admirable teacher. But before Beatrice knew it, she was opening her mouth and words were coming out. "Well, sir, I guess I have noticed that she can be rather flirty with the boys."

"*Flirty?*" Gerry turned.

"Flirty," said Beatrice, straight faced.

"Beatrice, if you don't mind, can you please elaborate on this point a little more for me?" Gerry sat back at his desk and got his pen.

An hour later, Beatrice walked out of Gerry's office and went to her empty classroom and packed her papers and textbooks and jacket and caught the next train back home. She had no special plans for the weekend but anyway she wanted to get the hell out of there as soon as she could.

Finals week came like a county fair. Beatrice was so proud of her students. To start the week, they gave her a framed photo of the class from their field trip to the Museum of Man and Nature in Munich as a gift. That made her smile.

The whole week had a buzzing energy that reminded Beatrice of her own time in school, the accomplishment and promise of it all, and Beatrice began to feel worse about herself. Sure, the Waldo Institute was a dump and most of the faculty were jerks and the food stunk and the weather was dreadful, but what about her? Who the hell was Beatrice? After what she did, she was probably the worst thing crawling around at Waldo. Beatrice felt worse with each passing day and her mind wandered when her kids weren't around to distract her.

What if Bernie were to get fired? Or worse? What if a student was to be affected? Could Beatrice live with herself? By Friday, she hadn't heard anything more about Bernie and she didn't want to ask Gerry. That afternoon, she forced herself to visit Bernie's classroom.

When Beatrice got there, the classroom looked empty. Beatrice called out Bernie's name, then walked in all the way and found Bernie near the back window by the storage closet, smoking a cigarette and blowing the smoke out over the courtyard in the direction of the city.

"I didn't know you smoked," said Beatrice.

Bernie laughed. "Why would you?"

"We survived, I guess. How was your finals week?"

Bernie turned. "A nightmare, and yours?"

"Not that bad," said Beatrice.

"They're investigating me, Beatrice. The whole board is investigating me, can you believe it?"

Beatrice felt her stomach turn. "What? What could they possible investigate you for?"

"It doesn't matter, this place is worse than the *Enquirer.*"

"We have to do something."

"Did Gerry come to talk to you about me?"

"What? No way."

"Just know that it's not true, if you hear anything." Bernie ashed her cigarette against the outside of the building then dropped the evidence into the rose bushes below.

"This is crap, I know you're a good teacher," said Beatrice.

"Oh, I'm a phony," said Bernie. "If you knew who I was back in Dallas, you wouldn't be saying that. I'm not Little Miss Perfect, I came here to start over."

"I don't believe you."

"What does it matter?"

"Everyone here loves you."

"Well, at this place, you can pretend to be whatever you

want."

"Bernie, do you hate me?"

"Hate you? Beatrice, I came here to get away from home and everything that reminded me of it. And that just so happens to include people like you."

"That's why I couldn't join your Overseas Club?"

"That and I find you pretty annoying sometimes."

Beatrice laughed to her own surprise. "Not the first time I've heard that."

Bernie shook her head. "Gosh, I'm sorry. Seriously. I shouldn't take this out on you. I don't know what's gotten into me lately. I know all of this has nothing to do with you."

"I'll try talking to Gerry, maybe I can help."

"Don't worry, I'm getting a lawyer." Bernie closed the window then went to her desk and began tidying up.

Beatrice stood and pretended to examine old notes on Bernie's whiteboard. "So did it work, running away here?" asked Beatrice.

"I've gotten so good at lying to myself, sometimes I can't tell," said Bernie. "I've made a lot of mistakes professionally and personally, it's just depressing that I seem to keep making the same ones."

"What do you mean?" asked Beatrice.

"That tall kid you saw in my class, Anton. He did, he does, have a crush on me. I let him walk me home a few times, I know I shouldn't have. People probably saw us together after school and that's all it took for the gossip to start flying. I invited him up to my flat a few times."

"Bernie, you don't have to tell me anything."

"Oh stop it, Beatrice. It's not like that. We just talked, he's an army brat like me, you know. And his mom is fooling around on his dad and it's devastating for him. I know from experience what he's going through. I mean, we're teachers, right? Aren't we supposed to guide these kids? Does that end as soon as the bell rings?"

"You're a good teacher, Bernie."

"Anyone who moves to the other side of the world to teach is a good teacher."

"In a few years, Anton will be a very handsome man."

"The legal age in Germany is sixteen."

"You're terrible," said Beatrice.

"I tried telling you." Bernie winked and went back to the window.

"You know Bernie, I think in another place and at another time, you and me could have been wonderful friends," said Beatrice.

Bernie smiled and shrugged then took out another cigarette.

When Beatrice left Bernie's classroom, she still felt awful about what she did but there was something about seeing Bernie like this, in this condition, that made Beatrice feel okay about the universe.

It was raining when Beatrice came in for her last day at

the Waldo Institute. With the mountains in sight, Beatrice told Gerry that she would not be returning for another year and that she had lied for no good reason about Bernie and that the rumors he had heard about Bernie were probably just that, rumors. Beatrice told Gerry that Bernie was an exceptional teacher. Gerry was confused and quite angry but he said he appreciated her honesty. Still, there was no way he could write her a letter of recommendation or pay for the cost of her return flight. Beatrice said that she understood.

Beatrice left the Waldo Institute and the country without saying goodbye to anyone, including Bernie.

The flight home was twelve hours.

Beatrice had a lot of time to think on the airplane. She knew that life was about experiences, collecting them and using them to build upon who you were as a human and who you wanted to be on this planet. Maybe sometimes you didn't recognize what you learned during the experience, only afterward. Beatrice hoped so.

Through the window, Beatrice looked down at the Black Forest far below, sprawling hills and valleys and plains, a patchwork of dark greens and browns and occasional splashes of yellows and whites, hiding another world beneath its canopy.

Beatrice knew one thing for certain. She would start her own Overseas Club. There must be lots of international people in Bakersfield. She would share her authentic Eintopf recipes and explain the delicate nuances between European and American culture and explain the more complex rules of *Fußball*, or soccer, and she would be a fair president that would let anyone join the club, even if they had never been overseas or were annoying or awkward or had bad manners.

When Beatrice returned from the restroom, the cabin was dark and most of the passengers were already sleeping, but the elderly Indian-looking lady next to her seemed to want to talk.

"How did you enjoy Germany?" asked the stranger.

"Actually, I've lived there the past year," said Beatrice.

"Oh, how exciting, did you absolutely adore it?"

Beatrice smiled politely and nodded, then put her headphones back on and ignored the old woman as she resumed watching her movie, the latest garbage out of Hollywood, before eventually falling asleep to the dips and soft rumbles of the Boeing 747 as it cruised over the Atlantic.

GORY SPECIAL

Easy does it, Marv. Start slow. Like we practiced. Grapple, arm drag to chicken wing, snapmare reverse, follow up rear choke, side headlock into Miss Patel's fence, clothesline duck on one, hip toss, clothesline duck on two, surprise elbow, double clothesline on three, double kick up, pose and wait. Always wait. This is where the crowd goes wild, two perfectly matched technicians inside the squared circle, an opening exchange hinting at a classic match just getting started.

Babyface makes me the face, beard, however sparse, makes Marv the heel. Good guy, bad guy. There's no crowd of course, but the psychology of the match is just as important. What separates real wrestling from a bunch of idiots slamming each other on a pile of mats in a backyard. Bird and Jerome's hardcore match today will get the most views on YouTube, but our match will get the most *likes*.

"*There's* the cheap shot!" shouts Stick, our announcer,

referee and cameraman, kneeling feebly by the tripod. "That mean streak we've been waiting for all day from Marvelous Marv!"

I pop my jaw. Marv is off the mark and his European uppercut catches. He's excited, agitated even, and that's a good thing. Wrestling is like theatre acting, you feed off each other.

"Great one," I whisper, away from camera. "Now the ribs."

Heels cheat. They're the bad guys, don't forget. Illegal holds, closed fists, isolating a single body part with extreme nastiness. As planned, Marv is targeting my ribs today. Hard knees, then a textbook gutwrench powerbomb, more juice than expected. I grunt.

Pin fall. Kick out. One count.

This is the last "pay-per-view" we're ever going to film. After summer, I'll go away to college and Marv will start driving for his dad's bread company. Morning deliveries, weekend shifts, yeast. Poor bastard. He should've paid more attention in class, I always told him. Not giving a damn only gets you points in high school, not the real world.

I rise gingerly, holding my side. My finishing move is the Pedigree, the double underhook facebuster popularized by Triple H, and I cannot perform this with busted ribs. And without a finisher, even the most casual fan knows, a wrestler is good as dead.

Marv, his finisher is the Gory Special, the standing

backbreaker submission invented by famed lucha libre Gory Guerrero. Marv never liked the mainstream guys like me. Sellouts, he calls them. He never had cable anyway to watch WWE or WCW. Once in middle school he made us go to an indie show at some crummy high school gym the next town over. Tickets were only ten bucks. My parents paid.

"Solid work, Marv," I whisper. "Now with the——"

"I know what the hell I'm doing," says Marv.

Marv elbows me in the ribs, hooks my arm, and lifts me high for a fallaway belly-to-back suplex. I hit the mat with a thud, a pack of ground meat dropped on the kitchen floor.

"What are you crazy fools doing over there?" shouts Miss Patel, suddenly peering over the fence. "Lucas! Where is your mother? At the wine bar again?"

Stick improvises with usual deftness. "You never know what to expect here at Intense Championship Wrestling, fans! Our show is raw, live and *uncut*!"

I tumble onto my knees and crawl to the fence. "Sorry, Miss Patel, we're just shooting a school project." My neighbor's eyes roll. She used to babysit me when I was little, but that was a long time ago.

When I stand and turn, Marv gives me a Nature Boy Ric Flair chop, loud and open handed, right across the chest. Even with a shirt on, it stings like hell.

One time freshman year, Marv's dad was really pissed at Marv for leaving the dog off the leash in the yard. He came and got Marv after baseball practice and smacked him around in front of the whole team. Marv has some of his dad in him. When he gets going, no one can tell him anything. But people respect that about Marv. I'm going to miss these small town stories when I'm at Berkeley. They'll probably get a kick out of them up there.

Marv grabs me by the mane. The attack continues as choreographed. Tilt-the-world gut buster followed by an elbow drop. Pin fall. Kick out. Two count. Sidewalk slam followed by a guillotine leg drop. Pin fall. Kick out. Two count again.

"You told Angela Darasouk I was a loser," says Marv. "Going to live and die in this town baking bagels?"

"Angela Darasouk?" I whisper, out of breath.

Once in eighth grade, Marv didn't talk to me for a week because I danced with Gloria Gardner at our Spring Formal. One lousy dance. To a Boyz II Men song. You'd think a guy Marv's size would be less sensitive about these sorts of things. Girls always liked him anyway. He never had to work for anything. Did Angela Darasouk really say something? I always told Marv to his face that he was an underachiever. He could do anything he wanted. Just because his family never went to college and rotted in this town, it didn't mean he had to.

"Don't know what you're talking about, Marv," I say, lips like a ventriloquist.

He pulls me up by the collar.

He winds up and unloads a big right hand.

I block it.

There's a point in every match where the good guy attempts a comeback, unsuccessfully. You see, it's too early. You must tease the crowd, delay what they want. So as I show signs of life, blocking another right hand then countering with a jab, I go for an epic, momentum-shifting, crowd-exciting suplex. But Marv kicks me in the groin, stopping me cold. I scrunch my face. He reverses and executes a big tiger suplex. We both bounce off the mat and remain on our backs, the signal for our mid-match breather.

We stare at the clouds, panting.

"Not that you'd understand, but I want to work for my dad," says Marv. "While you're up there drinking lattes and studying poetry, I'll be running a business."

"I'm sure you'll be calculating a lot of figures inside that crusty truck," I say.

Marv elbows me in the forehead.

"Ten, nine, *eight*..." hollers Stick as both men remain down.

"I didn't say anything to Angela Darasouk," I say. "Don't be stupid, you're like my brother."

"You're too small to be my brother."

"Three, two..." continues Stick.

"Up, Marv," I say. "Time for your cobra clutch."

Marv stands right as Stick calls out "one." He flips me over and locks me into the cobra clutch submission, a raised Boston crab, pulling my midsection, squeezing my throat. We both face the camera wonderfully. He growls, a wickedly good heel. I grimace, blood filling my neck, no acting required.

In college, I bet the girls will be different. They won't be petty gossip girls like Angela Darasouk. They will be sophisticated and progressive and worldly. They will probably be hot, too. There are plenty of fish in the sea, my dad always says. Marv can have Angela Darasouk, the loud mouth. She liked Marv more anyway.

My ribs begin to really hurt as Stick runs over for his first onscreen duties as referee. He lifts my hand to see if I'm still conscious. He delicately drops it. The thing hits the mat.

"One!" calls Stick. He lifts my hand a second time and releases. Thud. "*Two!*" Slowly, he lifts my hand a third time. If it falls again, the crowd well knows, this match is over.

Stick lets go. My hand falls. Like a dumbbell. But an inch from the mat, it stops. It forms a fist. It begins to shake violently.

This, people, is what they call a turning point.

"I don't believe it!" cries Stick. "Cool Hand Luke is not out of this match yet! The kid's got heart!"

I shake both my arms like a madman and stand, Marv still hanging off my back. This is where the crowd erupts. They want the face to overcome the heel. Wrestling is about reaffirming basic beliefs, not questioning them. And good guys win over bad guys.

Once upright, I spring backwards and drop Marv flat on his back. He gets up. I clothesline him. He gets up again. I drop kick him. He gets up once more, this time I wrap my arms around his neck and leap forward with a Diamond Cutter. We both land with a smack on the mat, limp, as planned, Marv from the attack, me from the exertion of my last-ditch offensive flurry. The crowd is on pins and needles. They don't know who has the edge now.

I wheeze. "Besides, you can't listen to a girl like Angela Darasouk."

Marv turns. "What?"

"You shouldn't listen to a girl like her, I'm saying."

Marv was always dramatic. You have to be cool, I always said. Girls don't like emotional guys. Girls don't like wrestling either. But this isn't about girls. We do this for us. Wrestling is about brotherhood, an intimate bond possible only through trust. There is no luck or chance. Did you know that wrestling is the only sport without an offseason? It airs every week, rain or shine. It's a snapshot in history, a moment between two men. Two warriors. It can never be recreated. It's something special.

And our match will be legendary. What all other backyard wrestling matches on YouTube are measured against. No missed spots. No over selling. No botches. Today's match has been perfect so far. A riveting yarn spun through bumps and holds. This will be our masterpiece. And this closing exchange will seal it.

I lock Marv into a classic collar and elbow tie up, our foreheads pressed, facing south. "Focus, Marv. We're almost there. We can talk later."

"Tell me what happened between you and Angela."

"Finish strong, Marv. This is our moment. In ten years, when I'm at some big firm in New York and you're stuck in traffic on a bagel delivery, we'll think about this day and smile."

"Get a life asshole, this isn't that serious."

Marv grunts and breaks the tie up, as heels should. He Irish-whips me into the fence. I return with a classic Lou Thesz press. Once on top, I start with the left fists, high and furious. Ten of them. The crowd chants along during this, of course. I climb the top turnbuckle, our sharp metal ladder, and jump off with a frog splash. He rolls out of the way, barely clearing it. I crash into the mat. We lie there again. It's getting hard to breathe.

"You don't even like her," I say.

"Tell me what happened," says Marv.

"Remember when you were obsessed with starting a band and Mr. Dumas finally let us use the music room for practice and you didn't show up once."

"And you showed up every day and still suck."

"You only like the idea of things."

"You just care about yourself."

Marv stands and yanks me with him.

"Did you guys screw?" asks Marv.

"What?"

Marv shoves me in the chest, far above my ribs. "Tell the truth for once in your life." He pulls me back in with a tight clinch.

"Fine." I squeeze my forearms. "You want to know?"

"I want to know."

"We made out last week at the pool. After Ben's birthday party."

Marv flexes, then lifts me sideways and releases me with a superb Samoan drop.

We both slap the mat loudly, our bodies getting heavier.

"The hatred between these two wrestlers is *palpable*!" shouts Stick. "It's hard to believe these men were once tag team partners, once *friends*! This is a grudge match!"

Bird and Jerome come out of the garage. Their hardcore match is next.

"Things happen," I say, gasping. "Don't be mad at me."

Marv spits into the dirt. "Know what? You're right," he whispers. "Let's finish strong. But not for you. For this, for the boys." He snarls ruthlessly for Bird and Jerome to see, then turns and roars directly into the camera.

Bird and Jerome cheer and whistle and holler.

We both pop up.

"I don't believe it," cries Stick. "These men are tougher than a two-dollar steak!"

Easy does it, Marv. Here we go.

It starts. Grapple, half nelson to full nelson, belly to back throw, back flip reversal, left kick miss, right kick miss, sit down jaw breaker, running clothesline duck on one, running clothesline duck on two, gut kick, double underhook into the Pedigree set up, pause, back body drop reversal, full flip reversal, turn, gut kick, inverted double underhook, clinch, spin, lift, right into the Gory Special set up.

This is where I will tap. I will resist with all my heart, but the brutal assault on my ribs earlier will prove to be too much. The heel, in an absolutely astonishing upset, will defeat the face and become the *new* Intense Championship Wrestling World Champion.

Marv launches me onto his back, arms still hooked, my hamstrings slung over his shoulders like a rollercoaster harness. He locks his wrists around my ankles and tightens, stretching my torso. It is perfect. I am a human ribbon, tied to the back of a wild boar.

The Gory Special is glorious.

"I can't believe my eyes!" shouts Stick. "The Gory Special is applied, it's only a matter of time before this match is over, folks!"

As I stare at the world upside down, I wonder if this will really be the last time we wrestle. I wonder how things will go after summer. I think about Marv and how much we've changed since third grade with Miss Guzman. I wonder if our friendship is something real, or just the byproduct of two kids liking similar things living in close proximity of one another. Perhaps now is simply a crossroads between two men meant to exist one way for the first seventeen years of their lives and another way for the next fifty. I wonder for some reason if Marv will be happier than me in life.

"I'm sorry, Marv," I whisper. "About Angela. I don't know why I did it."

As my spine bends, I wonder if I should tap.

Then Marv lets go.

I plunge to the mat, nearly falling on my neck.

What the hell are you doing, Marv.

This isn't what we practiced.

I roll over and struggle to one knee, confused and angry.

Marv picks up a folded steel chair from the corner. It's for Bird and Jerome's hardcore match, a ringside prop that looks good on camera but will never actually be used.

"Don't worry," says Marv. "Guys like us, we'll always be friends."

He swings. The crack of steel on skull startles every animal in the neighborhood. Bird and Jerome drop their pads and run on screen. Stick turns silent for the first time in his life. Miss Patel starts making noise as she bursts through the fence gate, screaming at an unimaginable pitch, asking what happened, threatening to call the police or ambulance or both. This is an even better ending than we planned, Marv. You bastard. What a last match, I think to myself, as the sun flickers and the earth tips gently.

BATHROOM BREAK

Noreen closed the bathroom door behind her. She was drunk. She stood in the mirror. Her face looked fat. Her cheeks were brioche buns and her jawline was a slab of pork belly. Hah! That was funny, thought Noreen. If she had a food blog, which people probably assumed about her all the time, that line would go great in a piece about how people and their favorite foods start to look alike, like pets and their owners. *Glazed Pork with Sweet Relish on Buttered Brioche Bun —Noreen P. from California.*

She had gained a few pounds this year, sure. Noreen had no problem with that. She had a scale and mirror but how she really knew she had gained weight was this: she hadn't heard a fat person joke in a long time. When she was skinnier, Noreen recalled, she would often hear the casual fat jokes that skinny people share freely in the company of one another. Now, she was officially the girl you shouldn't make fat jokes in front of.

Noreen ran cold water over her fingers. She pressed down along her cheekbones, a boxer being smeared with Vaseline between rounds. Her face was ruddy from rum and winter.

There was one semester in college when people thought she was gay. How did she come to know this? She didn't hear anything gay-related all spring. Finally, someone made an insensitive remark in front of her and quickly apologized. So, thought Noreen, maybe it was safe to assume that behind closed doors, skinny people said things about fat people, straight people said things about gay people, White people said things about Black people, dogs said things about cats? And vice versa?

Noreen messed with her hair. Damn split ends.

It would be a shame, thought Noreen, if overweight biracial rumored lesbians were privy to fewer insider jokes than, say, verified straight White males. Noreen loved a good politically incorrect joke. She could laugh at herself just fine. And others. She had thick skin. That pork belly fat. Hah!

What if her friends were talking about her outside *now*? No, they were good people. Open-minded and loving. She could probably get laid tonight if she wanted to. Yes, there were a few gentlemen here that could win a ticket to the rodeo—

"Shit or get off the pot already!" The old door rattled.

"Just a *minute*!" said Noreen. She could puke.

But guys didn't like skinny girls anyway. Girls didn't like skinny girls. Hell, only magazines liked skinny girls. And Hollywood. Same with blonde hair and blue eyes. Noreen had never met a person that actually *said* they liked blonde hair and blue eyes better. Was that just because it sounded too *Nazi*-ish? Or was it because people simply didn't say that in front of *her*? Maybe that's why she always heard people say they loved curves and brown eyes and that Black was beautiful. Was it okay to say White was beautiful? Red? Yellow?

Noreen collected water in her hands and drank, like a happy little duck. She felt better.

Why was she being mean to skinny people? That wasn't nice, thought Noreen. Not nice at all. Some people were skinny because of *disease*, for Christ's sake. A girl in her middle school had bulimia. Amy Bora. Poor Amy Bora. Throwing up her Lunchables behind the PE locker rooms. Where was Amy Bora now? Probably a supermodel somewhere, making millions of dollars. On a yacht. In Dubai. Wait a second, screw Amy Bora. Why should Noreen feel guilty? She was simply *thinking* these thoughts, after all. In a bathroom.

Yes, actually, Amy Bora could kiss her ass. Toss her salad for all she cared. Hah! Salad. Another food reference. There was an idea for a food blog entry: *10 Food-Themed Derogatory Insults*. Lick my cornhole. Snack on deez nuts. Eat shit and die. Wait, that last one didn't work.

Ugh, thought Noreen. She shouldn't drink so much. Come new year, she would drink less. Yes. And eat better. And spend less time online. And think nicer thoughts.

Noreen dried her hands. She would not puke. She left the light on and went back out to her friends in the little kitchen. They were painters and singers and readers and intellectuals and they talked a lot. But come to think of it, they didn't talk about art or Tibet or global warming. They talked about people, often those who were not in the room. They said mean things. They laughed.

As Noreen settled into her wooden chair and poured another rum, she felt better about the world. People were people. Yes, always were, always going to be. Behind closed doors, people just liked to talk and, well, what was so incredibly terrible about that?

STAR OF THE WORLD

It was toilet-seat-sticks-to-your-ass kind of weather and Hal wasn't having it. He left the bathroom window open and went into the bedroom to put on his favorite corduroys. Left leg, right. What a sticky, God-awful day. Was early November always like this? It was when Hal was a boy. Global warming wasn't real, just something the government suits cooked up for a laugh and a scare, keep the sheep baaaing like fools. Baaa. They used to say television could make you blind. Hal could still spot a great ass from a mile away. Like that new redheaded meter maid. Her kaboose was alright.

Hal turned off the TV and turned up the AC. Maybe the president was right. It was the Orientals that made up global warming. Keep us buying Japanese. Electric cars. Ha ha ha. If a man ever tried to take Hal's Ford Taurus, that poor fool would have a fun time explaining to his doctor why there was an old Louisville Slugger with the initials

H.L. shoved up his ass! If you asked Hal, that Elon Musk freak from the news could take his electric cars, and his spaceships for that matter, back to South Africa where he came from. Electric cars. Ha ha ha.

Hal finished his iced tea. Ahhh. Stuff from the stores was no good. All sugar. Hal placed the empty plastic glass in the sink and got his leather book bag. He was going to mail his daughter Fran a letter today. Hal looked at the clock on the stove. Where had the morning gone? He was late.

Hal shut his apartment door and shook the knob with force. He caught a glimpse of his face in the reflection on the lacquered wood. He looked old. That's what thirty years of repairing appliances at Montgomery Ward will do to a man, thought Hal. That store wasn't even around anymore. Just another forgotten relic from the past. Like Hal? No. Come on. Retirement and more free time than any man could know what to do with was reward for a lifetime of work. Hal made his contribution to civilization. It was fine if society and his old drinking pals and even his own daughter didn't need him much these days. He didn't need anyone, either.

Hal turned the deadbolt over until it clicked.

Anyway, looking old meant looking respectable. Grey hairs made him look like an old movie star. Like Harrison Ford. Right, thought Hal. A regular Han Solo. *I've got a bad feeling about this!*

The elevators were out. The elevators always went

out when the heat kept up. Hal's doctor said he should be walking more, his heart and all. Stairs were good. Though what did his doctor know? The kid looked like Doogie Howser. A little Indian Doogie Howser. Hal hadn't thought about that stupid TV show in years. His daughter Fran used to love that show. It was probably what made her decide to go to medical school in the first place. It certainly wasn't anything Hal passed down to her. Hal should ask Fran about it the next time he saw her. When would that be? After last year, certainly not Thanksgiving.

Hal turned the corner and descended onto the second floor. The Jackson Boy was just coming up. "Hey, pops." He nodded at Hal without looking up from his screen.

Jesus. Headphones, cell phone, video game thingy, sunglasses, blinky watch. That boy needed help. When Hal was the Jackson Boy's age, his father taught him that a man only needed three things when he left the house: his wallet, his comb, his knife. Advice like that never really translated right to a daughter.

Hal finally got outside. Holy Toledo. It was ten times hotter than inside. And the sound of the city was as bad as the heat. Buses, jackhammers, strange foreign languages. Even after living in his apartment in the city for three years, Hal couldn't get used to the noise. On days like today, he missed the suburbs. But he sure didn't miss Susan. Or Gwen after that. Witches. The whole lot of them. He'd take noise and loneliness any day over those doll-faced dictators.

Gwen tried to stop by unannounced the other day to see if Hal needed help with things. Hal knew better than to answer the buzzer for that sneaky sorceress.

East. The post office was west but Hal wanted to eat lunch first and the new chicken sandwich place was two blocks east. The grub there wasn't bad. Not bad at all. In fact, pretty damn tasty. Though what did *halal* mean? It didn't matter. Their early bird senior's special lasted until 11:30 a.m. Free salad or wedges with any sandwich. Mmmm.

Only ten minutes left. Where did the time keep running off to? Hal was losing track of it more and more these days. He picked up the pace and walked faster.

Soon Hal could drive places again. He was a fine driver. A regular Michael Schumacher. Hal told Fran and the DMV lady this multiple times. But at Hal's age, you now had to renew your driver's license in person. It was law. Was it the president's idea? It was discrimination if you asked Hal. *Hell no, we won't go!* Hal would take it to the street like the silly hippies in the old days. Fran always said Hal should take more interest in social justice. That was something he and Fran could always count on disagreeing about. It was simple if you asked Hal, anything in this country was possible with a little grit and elbow grease. Everyone was responsible for their own individual well-being—

A car honked then skidded into the crosswalk. Christ! Hal jumped back onto the curb. "*Damn* it, old man!"

The driver in the silver suit gave Hal the finger and Hal instinctively started shouting back. Hal wasn't sure what exactly he was shouting, but the threats tumbled out loud and steady. Muscle memory. Hal then stormed right up to the driver's open window.

Some teenagers by the bus stop took out their phones and started recording. The driver mumbled something about "crazy" and "psycho" and peeled out on the green light. Chicken shit. Men today always liked starting things they couldn't finish. Hal would have pounded that yuppie into the pavement.

Hal got back on the curb and waited for the light. He waited for his heart rate to come down. The teenagers were still filming him. What was this, a reality TV show? Hal waved them away, as if motion might somehow power down their devices. The teenagers just giggled and eventually put their phones away, bored.

Green. Hal walked.

The smell of scorched rubber hung in the air.

This whole world was going insane. Who let that reckless driver loose on the streets? Who let these teenagers loiter like criminals? No one had any respect anymore. How were you supposed to have respect for others when they had none for you? Maybe there were no real causes to care about anymore. People were bored and numb. Maybe everyone just wanted to sit back comfortably and watch the world crumble.

Last summer, Fran showed Hal a website called World Star. A boy at her hospital showed it to her. The website posted videos every day of car crashes and mean pranks and fist fights on the street. For fun. Entertainment. It was terrible. Fran showed Hal a video of one kid slamming another kid on a curb while a group of more kids watched. These days, it seemed people didn't break up fights or go get help, they simply chanted "*World Star*! *World Star*!" and filmed the whole thing like perverts. Sick perverts. At least that was one thing Hal and Fran agreed on.

Oh baby, right on time. 11:25 a.m. Hal made it. He walked inside Haziz's Halal Chicken Shack. There was just a young man in line, dressed in an oversized white denim jacket and matching white jeans hanging nearly off his ass. Hal didn't understand fashion these days.

Hal got in line behind Denim Man. Hal scanned the menu but he didn't need to. Chicken Combo Sandwich with white sauce. Plus, that free order of wedges. And what the heck, a small coffee if it came with free refills.

Hal smacked his lips. Ready. Though what was taking so long? There was just one college girl with piercings at the cash register. She had greenish hair and kind eyes under all that black eye makeup. She reminded him a bit of Fran at that age, rebellious but sweet. The Denim Man asked Piercing Girl dumb question after dumb question, even though he was already holding his bag of food. What the hell was he doing? Flirting with the poor girl? Hal looked at his watch.

"This isn't a singles bar," said Hal loudly. "Are you going to take your damn food or what?"

"Is this guy serious?" Denim Man turned around.

Hal clenched his fist, nervous but ready. "You're holding up the line."

Denim Man looked Hal up and down, then at the invisible line behind him, and laughed. "You're lucky you're old, grandpa." The man took his bag of food and said to Piercing Girl, "I'll get that number later, baby girl."

Denim Man turned around and stared down Hal. Was he going to punch Hal? Hal had a chin. He could take a punch. Hal wasn't scared. He wasn't scared of the man.

Denim Man fake lunged. Hal flinched. Denim Man laughed all the way out the door. Hal unclenched his fist. His body was shaking. Goddamn it. Hal wouldn't have flinched years ago. His fist was a rock years ago. If only Hal was younger, he could have knocked that cowboy out. He would've served him a sandwich himself. A hot and fresh knuckle sandwich.

Hal exhaled once more and waited for his heart rate to come down again.

He stepped up to the counter and ordered.

"Okay, one chicken combo sandwich, wedges and a small coffee. That's $9.85," said Piercing Girl.

"Wait," said Hal. "Wedges are free with the early bird special."

"I'm sorry sir, but you're late." Piercing Girl looked

at the clock. "It's 11:33 a.m. and the early bird special is over. I'm really sorry, I've already gotten in trouble once for bending the rules."

"I got here on time!" said Hal. "It was your boyfriend that held up the line."

"That creep was not my boyfriend." Piercing Girl looked out the window. "Tell you what sir, my manager's out on her smoke break. It's no problem, let me just give you the wedges."

"Give me the wedges? I don't need your charity. Pack up the chicken sandwich, nothing else."

"I'm really sorry," said Piercing Girl one more time.

Hal ate alone by the window. The place was empty except for another senior citizen, but Hal didn't like hanging out with other old geezers. Anyway, the guy looked senile. Hal ate calmly and watched the cars outside. The chicken sandwich didn't taste as good as it did the last time he was here. Oh, nothing of good quality lasted very long in this world. He eventually finished the sandwich and crumpled up the foil wrapper into a silver nugget. He took the tray to the trash can. He was thirsty but he refused to give another penny to this gypsy camp. He could drink his iced tea at home.

Hal left the restaurant through the side doors.

West. It was three blocks back west to the post office. The post office closed at noon on Saturdays. Five minutes to go. Damn. Hal was always a few minutes behind it seemed.

At least walking was good after lunch. That's what Indian Doogie Howser might say right about now.

Hal thought about Fran as he crossed the street. He used to take her into the city every Sunday when she was little. She loved it. Fran used to look up to her father. Hal was her hero. It was easy to impress children, thought Hal. It was harder to impress adults. Was Fran still impressed by her father? Hal didn't think so. Why should she be? There was nothing left in this world he could give her. No knowledge, no money, not even conversation anymore. But Hal was impressed by his daughter. He was. A doctor. Christ. Never in a million years. Hal should tell Fran how proud he was of her more often.

Hal forgot to look both ways and stepped off the curb. A car came to a safe stop and the driver gave Hal a friendly wave from a distance, go ahead. Hal waved back.

Maybe it was Hal that had gone crazy, not the world. The truth was, everything had changed so much. Maybe Hal hadn't changed enough. Maybe Hal hadn't changed at all. Maybe the world had whizzed right by him. Maybe that's how Hal became a forgotten relic, why nobody needed him anymore. Who wanted a Model T when you had electric cars?

Hal got to the other side of the street. Oh, maybe the only thing left for Hal to do on this planet was live out his final days in solitude and die quietly under the porch steps. There you go, Hal. That was the spirit!

11:59 a.m. The post office was still open and it wasn't too crowded. Hal walked inside and a pleasant mail lady showed him where he could get in line before they closed. As he waited, Hal took out Fran's birthday card from his leather bag and read it before sealing the envelope.

Francine,

Happy 30th birthday. I hope it is a good one.

When will you take me to the DMV? You said you would. Keep your word you are an adult. And when will you transfer me more money? I am not gambling anymore but my pension is so low you know. You are the rich doctor help your poor dad okay? Don't tell your mother. Transfer it before December okay? I am walking more. My heart is good. I have been watching a lot of movies lately. Richard Pryor is funny do you know him?

My computer is still broken. Please come fix again.

Sincerely,
Father

Great, thought Hal. Fine.
Seal it. Stamp it. Send it.
After giving the clerk the envelope, Hal headed toward the exit. On his way out, he passed a box of vintage Tin Tin

stamps sitting on a glass display. Fran used to love that little Belgian boy and his dog. Hal should buy a box for Fran. Though at $11.80, what the hell was Uncle Sam trying to pull? Hal picked up a box anyway and got back in line to pay. Fran would be happy to see Tin Tin. It was worth it. He could call Fran later. If she picked up, Hal could tell her about the Tin Tin stamps and even ask if he could come by the house this week to give them to her.

The sun was high when Hal got outside. It was the hottest the day would get. Hal's shirt and underwear were soaked through. Hal started walking back to his apartment. It was normally a good feeling to accomplish everything you had set out to do in the day, but today it didn't feel good. Hal felt restless inside. The remainder of his day was open but there was nothing for him to do. Nothing at all.

Well, he could walk the long way through the park, Hal finally decided. Yes. Great. And once he got home, he could take a nap. After that, he could cook and eat dinner, maybe fish fillets and potatoes. Then he could watch a movie before bed, maybe something with Harrison Ford. Perfect. It wasn't much of a plan, but it was what he had.

As Hal turned toward the park, he heard noises by the bus stop. There were people standing around.

"Get off!" Shouted someone. "Psycho!"

Hal went toward the noises.

A crowd of people, mostly teenagers, was watching a man and woman argue. The man and woman were also sort of fighting. The man had his hands around the woman's wrists and she was kicking him where she could. He was just laughing.

Hal recognized them. It was Denim Man and Piercing Girl from Haziz's Halal Chicken Shack. Piercing Girl was wearing a windbreaker over her uniform now. Denim Man was no longer carrying his bag of food.

What were these other idiots at the bus stop doing, watching a matinee show?

"Someone get this creep off me," said Piercing Girl, twisting and kicking again wildly.

Hal got through the crowd.

Denim Man turned and immediately saw Hal. Denim Man shook his head. "You again, grandpa? Mind your business this time before you get hurt."

"Can you help me?" asked Piercing Girl.

"I didn't know the rodeo was in town," said Hal.

A kid in the crowd laughed.

"What?" asked Denim Man.

"Back in my day, we called your outfit a Canadian tuxedo," said Hal.

Denim Man let go of Piercing Girl's wrists. He fixed his collar and adjusted his belt. Hal let go of his leather book bag. This time Denim Man wasted no time with silly flinching or staring. Denim Man took a step right toward Hal and swung at his head.

Hal shot up his left forearm, partially out of instinct,

partially out of sheer panic, and something surprising happened. Hal blocked the Denim Man's punch.

Oooh went the crowd. Ahhh.

Hal grabbed Denim Man's arm by the wrist and yanked it down toward his waist, like a young tree branch.

Denim Man tried to swing now with his left arm. Hal performed the same maneuver, blocking the punch, then yanking the left arm down low. Hal had total control over Denim Man. He had him securely by both wrists. Under his baggy clothes, Denim Man was actually kind of puny and weak. Maybe Hal was stronger than he thought.

Hal carefully tugged the man left, then right, then down to one knee. The whole crowd laughed and cheered. Then Hal heard it. "*World Star!*" And from another giggling teenager, "*World Star!*" Hal got Denim Man down to both knees and then onto his chest. The man was flat on the sidewalk now. Hal then sat squarely on Denim Man's back, keeping his weight over the thick middle part. He rested his feet on each side of Denim Man's head.

Hal was panting like crazy. It wasn't going away. Was his heart going to give out? Was this how Hal was going to kick the bucket? No. Inhale. No way, thought Hal. Exhale. He felt healthy. Hal felt good. Hal slowed his breathing and finally relaxed his body. He looked around. Everyone was still filming.

"Jesus!" said Hal. "Someone use one of those damn things to call the police!"

Someone did.

The Piercing Girl grabbed her belongings and left the scene without saying a word to anyone. She probably had to get back to work, thought Hal. He watched her leave. She really looked like Fran the way she walked, eyes down and with purpose. She appeared physically uninjured at least. Hal checked his jacket pocket to make sure the Tin Tin stamps weren't destroyed. They were fine.

Hal wanted to follow Piercing Girl and make sure she was really okay but he was needed where he was. He had to restrain Denim Man until the police arrived. They would certainly want to talk to Hal about what happened. They would probably need to file a report. Hal was a witness. Or more like an active participant. Hal would be happy to give the police a detailed account of what happened. Plus, there were all those cell phone videos. Maybe one of them would end up online and Fran would see it. Hal kind of hoped so. Denim Man squirmed beneath him. Hal sunk his ass deeper into his spine. The crowd still watched. Maybe a reporter would come and want to interview Hal. For tomorrow's paper. Or better yet, for the six o'clock news. Yes, probably. Hal was a famous star now. Ha ha ha.

THE LONG WEEKEND

They were whispering about something juicy, Hank just knew it. Miss Shasky balanced on her tippy toes as she looked up at her tree of a boss, nodding only here and there. Hank watched them both through the square window on the door, through the glass with the metal wire grid magically pressed inside. He had stayed up all night again, drinking tea and watching old episodes of *Miami Vice,* and he was tired, eventually too tired to pay any more attention.

He returned his focus to the waffle bottoms of his shoes which had day-old mud caked into the rubber pretty good. They belonged to his brother Todd, but the soles still had plenty of grip. Hank began picking and scratching, well-positioned to do so sitting Indian style on the carpet like everyone else.

Little Miss Shasky tiptoed back into the classroom followed by Principal Baumhaus whose cropped brown hair swung above her torso like palm leaves.

"Quiet, everyone," said Miss Shasky before exiting softly stage left.

"Somebody had a very *busy* long weekend," announced Principal Baumhaus. "I just got off the phone with several parents as well as the police—well, campus ambassador Officer Escondido. It seems somebody here at Amelia Earhart has decided to misuse the student telephone directory."

Murmurs erupted among the thirty-two sixth graders. Hank snuck a glance across the room at his best friend Stanley whose puffy morning eyes grew big.

"Fifty prank calls in all were made to students of this school. Today I'll be meeting with each student, one by one, to see if we can't match the voice." Principal Baumhaus observed the speechless room before adding, "Unless, of course, the culprit wants to save everybody the time and come to my office to talk *privately*. Good day, Miss Shasky."

Hank's knees, below his elbows, began to shake.

Saturday night, Stanley had come by for a sleepover. Hank's parents had recently finalized their divorce and his mom thought it would be a good idea to have a friend stay over during what would be Hank's first dadless weekend. Hank's mom left for her night shift at the airport at nine, leaving the two boys alone in the house.

Opening the student directory was Stanley's idea but Hank made most of the calls. They learned quickly that

Hank had the one quality essential for any good prank calling—commitment. No matter what voice he took on or how agitated his victims became, Hank played his part furiously through to the end, never breaking character. Something came over him and before the sun came up he had prank-called an impressive assortment of friend and foe, from Aaron Archego to Beverly Yee.

Morning recess could not come fast enough for Hank and as he ran to the far tetherball court, he could count only three students pulled from class so far. Stanley and Kumar were starting a game when Hank arrived out of breath.

"Can you believe all the drama this morning, boys?" asked Kumar, smacking a hell of a serve.

"Stan, we need to see the principal," said Hank.

"No way in hell! We just became legends," said Stanley, hitting the ball with a single hammer fist.

"Baumhaus was talking about you two goobers?" asked Kumar.

"What if the police trace my phone line or something?" asked Hank.

"Hah! You really think the pigs are involved?" Stanley huffed and doublefisted a good one. "And that's another thing, you think Big n' Tall Baumhaus is really going to meet five-hundred students today?"

"Why didn't you two prank call my house?" asked Kumar.

"Must've slipped our minds."

"I'm serious, Stan. My mom's going to kill me."

"Oh, she's got other things to worry about."

"We should turn ourselves in before lunch."

"If you go and squeal, I'm going to have to tell Baum-haus and everyone else the truth." Stanley untangled a mistimed ball and turned to his naïve friend. "That you made those prank calls. It was your house and your phone, remember?"

Hank watched Stanley resume the game. After a few hard blows, Kumar finally used his height to his advantage and before long the yellow leather ball made one last clang against the metal, wound high and tight around the aluminum pole.

The bell rang.

"Don't worry, Hank," said Kumar. "You'll get first game next recess."

Lunch came as normal and Hank could now count nine students pulled from class. The whole morning had a dream-like quality and Hank struggled to remember if he had drawn Winston Churchill or Joseph Stalin for his biography assignment. In the cafeteria he avoided Stanley and sat by the flag with Shy Guy, who wasn't that quiet but the name had stuck. Hank ate his chimichanga and tater tots and fruit cup in relative solitude and wondered if the food at county juvenile hall would be any better. He thought about running away before Baumhaus got to him and if he could install plumbing in the treehouse he would

VINCENT CHU

build in this abandoned lot of land he knew about on the edge of town. He imagined what his mom would say when she found out. He imagined what his dad would say. He thought about his older brother Todd.

To avoid the herd, Hank left the cafeteria early and finished his cream soda outside by the water fountains.

"I went in to see the big Baumhaus," said a girl nearby. "Don't worry, I didn't say nothing."

Hank turned toward the bleachers. There was Beverly Yee. Hank sucked on his cream soda until it made a noise.

"And why would *I* be worried?" said Hank.

"Because *you* were the prank caller," said Beverly.

"If you think *I* was the prank caller, then why didn't you tell Principal Baumhaus?"

Beverly shrugged and hopped down a row, her neon hoop earrings jumping, too. "My mom was totally convinced it was a girl's voice on our answering machine. But I could recognize it was you, Hank."

"Why would someone want to prank-call you anyway, what would they even say?"

"Well, you left a message saying that you were Doctor Butkus, from the hospital, and that a huge mistake had been made because I was really born a boy. There was a botched circumcision but luckily you found the penis eleven years later. *So Mr. Yee, if you want to bring your daughter Beverly in to become a boy again, it's not too late. We can sew the penis right back on. We've even looked up new boy names for you. Beverly can now be Beavis or Bilbo. Please call the hospital tomorrow to make an appointment and pick the name."*

Hank started to laugh and so did Beverly.

"You sounded like a very believable woman doctor," said Beverly.

"My dad says my voice'll probably change next year," said Hank.

"Has it gotten weird yet, with your dad gone?"

"Oh, what are you yapping about now?"

"Relax, your mom tells my mom everything. It's not such a big deal, my old man moved out two years ago and now I get two Easters and two birthdays. Sometimes, between them, orthodontist appointments even slip through the cracks."

"That's great."

"In Paris, you know, couples don't even get married. They just make love and French kiss and raise babies, together or not. They don't even understand our notion of dating. As a culture, I think we should strive to be more like that."

"You've got all the answers, don't you?"

"Me and my mom are coming to your house for dinner Friday night. Your mom invited us, we're bringing meatloaf. My mom already bought the ketchup."

"Fine," said Hank.

The two-ton double doors broke open and on came the steer, caffeine and corn syrup already in the blood. Hank and Beverly carefully rejoined the student body and walked back to class together. Hank liked meatloaf.

It was during SSAR, Silent Sustained Afternoon Reading, that Hank came to a sudden and obvious conclusion. He was not going to see Principal Baumhaus after all. This logical decision came as Hank sat on the rug near the beanbags and pretended to read John Grisham's *The Rainmaker*, which he really had been reading for the past two months, at least as well as any eleven-year old could read a John Grisham novel, while secretly observing the classroom and watching only three more students pulled from class within the hour.

What a farce. Stanley was right, 500 students in one day was not happening. And anyway, why should Hank care? He didn't feel bad. Really. There were worse things in the world than a few stupid telephone calls. If you asked him, there were plenty of jerks at Earhart that could use a good ball-busting. Besides, some of the calls were pretty damn funny.

Todd would have had a good laugh if he heard them, thought Hank. Hell, if his brother were home, he probably would have made a few calls himself. Hank remembered when Todd and his dad used to mess with the drive-thru workers at Wendy's, using funny voices and asking silly questions like which part of the chicken their nuggets came from or if they could make round beef patties instead of their signature square ones. Hank was young then but he would watch from the back seat and it would bust him up every time.

Kumar kept his word, as he usually did, and during afternoon recess Hank got first game.

On his way back to class, Hank was relieved he had somehow missed Stanley on the playground. It was right about that moment that a cold wet finger entered his ear.

"What the—!"

"We need to speak," said Stanley.

"So speak!" whispered Hank.

Stanley yanked Hank behind the green handball wall, blocking them from the view of classroom windows.

"You can chill, Stan. I decided I'm not going to see Baumhaus."

"No shit, Sherlock."

"What, you can read my mind now?"

"The case is already closed, genius. Get this, Principal Baumhaus thinks Nate Ramsey made the prank calls—all of them. They're going to call his parents together right after school today!"

"Nate Ramsey?"

Nate Ramsey was about a foot taller than the other kids and already had hair on his chin. There were two ongoing rumors about Nate Ramsey. One was that he was really fourteen and held back several years for assaulting a former PE teacher. The other was that he could run a five-minute mile. If you asked any student at Earhart, they believed at least one of the two.

"Why Nate Ramsey?" asked Hank.

"Why do you think? Nate Ramsey is responsible for half the dirt that goes on around this dump."

"I thought you wanted us to become legends?"

"We will! Nate Ramsey takes the fall now, and next year when we go to Lincoln, we spread the word it was really us."

"Nate Ramsey will vaporize us."

"With his grades, he's getting shipped off to Chipman."

The second bell rang.

"See you at the bike corral after school?" asked Hank.

"Can't, my mom's picking me up early today for a haircut."

The two tardy boys ran back to class.

The last hour of the day was as foggy as the first for Hank. There was something about earthquakes and seismic belts and the San Andreas fault, then it was 2:50 and the bell was ringing. Every student in Miss Shasky's sixth grade class was free to leave, including Hank.

Outside, he walked so slowly to the bicycle corral that when he got there most of the bikes were already gone. He waited for someone, anyone, to come from behind and snatch him by the collar. But it never happened.

Hank found his yellow Mongoose and took off the chain.

"Bye bye, Doctor *Butkus!*" shouted Beverly as she

whizzed past toward the parking lot.

"Beverly, wait!"

She skidded to a stop, shooting gravel in every direction.

"When you saw Principal Baumhaus this morning, what did she ask you?" asked Hank.

Beverly turned and grinned. "She asked me which song I'm singing for the Winter Talent Show. Didn't you hear? Every performer had to go see her today."

A car honked. "Until tomorrow, Hank the Tank."

Hank watched Beverly sprint to her mom's blue Camry and tumble into the back seat. After a few minutes, Hank put the lock back on his bike.

By the time Hank showed up at Principal Baumhaus's door, he had already written the note and prepared a ribbon of Scotch tape. The school was mostly quiet by now except for Joe the Custodian who always shuffled around until four. In big letters, Hank's note read:

NATE RAMSEY IS INNOCINT.

Hank estimated that it would take one second to press the ribbon against the door and another one to press the note onto the ribbon. It was a long run back to the bicycle corral but he only needed to make it around the corner to be unseen—and that would take another three seconds; this meant five seconds total. As Hank calculated this, he realized that he had been standing in front of Principal

Baumhaus's door for nearly a minute already. He shook his limbs loose, stretched his shoulders, and slowly reached out his hand.

The door opened.

It was Principal Baumhaus.

"Hello there, Hank," she said with a smile. She looked shorter than normal. She wasn't wearing any shoes.

"Hi, Principal Baumhaus."

"Oh, don't mind my feet. I always do my stretches around this time."

Hank balled his fists.

"Hank, I was hoping I'd see you today."

Hank laughed quietly. "Why is that."

"I wanted to ask how your Veterans Day went yesterday. That was a beautiful memorial for Todd. Your mother put together something really special, you know. There was a whole story about it in the paper this morning, didn't you read it?"

Hank shook his head.

"Oh, I'm sure your mom will show you the minute you get home. It's difficult to think it's been two years already. Fighting for something you believe in is, well, it's heroic— you understand that, don't you Hank?"

He nodded his head as he always did to that kind of comment.

"You know, your brother Todd used to turn this school upside down."

"I never heard anything."

"It was a long time ago, a different time back then. But between you and me, that boy was a hellraiser." Principal Baumhaus laughed and ruffled Hank's hair. "Once, your brother Todd snuck into the girl's bathroom early in the morning and put clear plastic wrap over all of the toilets—beneath the toilet seat but above the bowl. I can't tell you how many poor little girls came screaming into my office drenched that morning!"

Hank smiled. That was way more creative than some prank calls.

"We all miss him, Hank. Dearly. The truth is, it's always hardest for the parents. I can only imagine. But that's why you have to be strong for them Hank, like a little support beam."

"My dad didn't want to go yesterday."

"I can understand, Hank. There's nothing wrong with that, we all deal differently. Your father is coming next month to volunteer at our year-end fundraiser. I'm very happy about that and I very much look forward to catching up with him."

"Where's Nate Ramsey?"

"Nate Ramsey? Heck, your guess is as good as mine. But home, is where I'm sincerely hoping."

Hank looked down at his shoes, the rubber toe was peeling. He would have to go to the shoe repair store at the mall this week.

Principal Baumhaus watched him. "You know, Hank, next year at Sutherby they have a morning campus radio show. I think you'd be perfect for it. In fact, I already mentioned your name to Principal Gomez over there."

"Principal Gomez?"

"Oh, it's nothing crazy. Just some quick news, announcements, comedy skits even—you know, the usual. You're great at that kind of thing, going off the cuff, really committing to a performance."

Joe the Custodian rolled on by, his big plastic bin almost full.

"It's getting late, Hank. Won't your mother pick you up?"

"I rode my bike."

"Well, I should wrap up a few things here before I hit the road. I'll never understand why, but traffic is always so screwy after a long weekend." She sighed dramatically. "So Hank, is there anything else you wanted to talk to me about?"

Hank shook his head.

"Nothing at all?"

Hank shook his head again.

"It's okay, Hank. You can tell me."

Hank looked up then down the hall. It was just the two of them.

"Go on, Hank."

"Principal Baumhaus…"

Hank looked up, making eye contact with his principal for the first time in the conversation.

"Thanks for the talk."

Principal Baumhaus opened her mouth to say something.

"Maybe tomorrow you can tell me another funny story about Todd," said Hank.

Principal Baumhaus nodded, then smiled.

Hank sprinted off in the direction of the bicycle corral, making it around the corner in under two seconds flat. The school day was over. If he rode fast enough, he would make it home in time to watch *Dukes of Hazzard*.

HANSARING

If they could make it to Hansaring, they would be fine. If they could make it inside the cinema, to the movie they had said all month they would definitely go see, find two seats somewhere in the middle not too close to the screen, sit in the dark for two hours and not talk, they would be good. They would walk out afterward themselves, a young man and young woman still happy to be in the company of one another. Dean was confident of this.

They didn't fight anymore, Dean knew, they simply stopped talking for long periods of time. So long, in fact, they eventually stopped wondering what the other was thinking—at least Dean did. And that was the trick, he knew, waiting it out. To be able to resist the urge to speak too soon—that was paramount. Too much communication could ruin a relationship; yes, past experience and his parents taught Dean this. So as they got on the train and found two vacant seats side by side near the middle doors,

Dean looked straight ahead and not at Henriette, turning his attention, with equal parts performance and genuine curiosity, to the strangers around them.

It was seven stops to Hansaring.

The man across from Henriette read a book. It was a very big book, a *Hunger Games* or *Game of Thrones* kind, with a sword and flame and chess piece on the cover. Dean had never read such a big book. The man was on the very last page and Dean felt guilty suddenly for spying on him during this personal moment, but he did not stop. It was not often, he reasoned, that he would get the opportunity to observe another person at the exact moment they finished a book, a big one at that. But, after the last page, the man, without so much as a satisfied nod or pensive stare, shut the thing and immediately put in his iPhone buds. This disappointed Dean.

The woman diagonal Henriette refused to smile. It was not necessary, of course, to smile on a city train, but Dean observed two funny things happen to her in as many stops, and both times she did not react. First, her friend, a taller lady, stood up to stamp her ticket when the doors opened and three fanatical teenage girls tumbled in, mid-conversation, crashing down on either side of the woman, before she had time to object. When the friend returned, the woman simply pointed matter-of-factly to the rambunctious girls to indicate that, by the friend's own fault for getting up, her seat had been taken. As the train jerked forward, the friend, still standing, rocked backwards and sat down with all her weight on a man's lap; that was the second funny thing that happened. The woman sitting watched with indifference, the way one might observe a stranger chewing on a fingernail. Dean decided he did not like watching this woman.

Outside, the park before the river passed on the right. As Dean watched the trees and joggers and drinkers through the glass, he looked at Henriette. Because she was also facing the window, he saw only her cheek, framed on one side by her black, beautifully straight hair.

Dean just then became aware that, to someone watching him and Henriette, they must seem like complete strangers. Or life partners. Any two people in between— coworkers, friends, acquaintances—would never go so long without speaking. This made Dean self-conscious and as he caught, what he believed to be, an elderly lady analyzing his and Henriette's situation, he almost spoke to Henriette right then and there, for no other reason than to present themselves more positively and truthfully to the public. But Dean resisted. Luckily, the elderly lady got off at the next stop.

A student in gym shorts took her place. He talked on his phone in another language, perhaps Turkish, at a polite and not unpleasant level. Dean listened for a while but then lost interest.

The next stop was Hansaring.

Dean and Henriette got off the train and walked onto

the escalator. When they got up to the street, they saw a crowd of people standing outside the cinema. Dean and Henriette crossed the road and walked side-by-side toward the glowing yellow lights. They did not hold hands, occasionally touching shoulders only when the pavement was uneven.

The movie was sold out.

Dean and Henriette remained there for a minute, among the other deliberating moviegoers. Dean scanned the marquis. There was another movie playing soon, but Dean knew it was one that Henriette would not want to see. Oh, the hell with it. This was getting ridiculous. He loved Henriette. He knew that, and he knew she knew that. They would get over this like they always did, and these fights, these prolonged periods of silence, the recent frequency of them, would come to pass like a fad, like last summer when they started making their own pickles. Anyway, enough time had passed. And if it hadn't, Dean knew, if anything from the movies, a change of setting could help convey the passing of time, so now that they were on the street, not on the train or in their hotel room, it might at least feel like enough time had passed to resume speaking. Yes, Dean could talk to Henriette again. He was sure of it.

"Should I buy us tickets for the new *Fast and the Furious* then?" asked Dean.

"Dean," said Henriette, turning to face him for the first time all night, water in her eyes. "We need to talk."

THE TENDERLOIN

The smell of urine was almost unbearable but by the corner it passed, replaced by the smell of wet vegetables on the curb. The restaurants, hip ethnic ones included, had closed up shop and pulled shut their iron accordion gates and it was getting to about that time in the night when the population shifted and the faces changed and the passers-through became outnumbered by the all-nighters. The street was freshly coated in the first rain of summer and with it came all the smells that had baked into the concrete during June. The piss and bok choy were just surface-level, Dean knew, the real smells would need until morning to be reactivated—if the rain kept on.

Even with a few in him, Dean kept his head low and walked fast, his fists deep inside a blue workman's jacket that was just humble enough not to draw additional attention. He liked to believe that, on a good day, he could pass for a drifter or weekend junkie and he felt a sense of pride whenever he walked past a bum and wasn't pressed for change or conversation, though deep down he knew he wasn't fooling anyone.

As Dean turned onto Eddy, his thoughts came back to Henriette. Three years, he reminded himself. A drunken one-night stand was worse than an ongoing affair, Dean told himself, it suggested impulse and desire, attraction. Dean caught himself thinking these thoughts and immediately removed them from his head, an act he had been performing with greater and greater ease as the evening went on.

Dean stopped at the liquor store before arriving at All Star Donuts and Chinese Food. He had called Bud rather out of the blue and anyway, Dean knew, it was always polite to bring something when meeting a friend.

Bud sat at a window booth, a rain jacket around his bathrobe and a donut and two tall boys already on his table. He stood when Dean walked in.

"There he is," said Bud.

"How are you, old pal?" asked Dean. He pulled out two more tall boys, Country Clubs, from a paper bag and added them to the table.

"You're a fine friend," said Bud.

"Kampai." Dean cracked open his can. He pulled off his jacket which was soaked through, he had been walking for longer than he expected to.

"What are you doing slumming these parts?" asked Bud.

"I met a coworker for a drink. Then took a walk. This place clears my head," said Dean.

"This place. It does something for everyone. Take take take, you got to give, brother. Eventually everyone gives something to the Tenderloin."

An underslept woman with silver hair appeared at their table.

"Order something," said Bud.

Dean wasn't planning to eat but it would be rude to drink for free. "A bear claw, please."

The woman said nothing and disappeared behind the counter.

"Problems with Henriette again?" asked Bud.

"No," said Dean. As much as Dean wanted to talk about Henriette, it was a long, unrevelatory story and he knew it wouldn't help matters. Anyway, that's not why he called Bud tonight.

"If you dragged me out of bed at this hour to piss and gripe about this poor woman again—"

"We're fine," said Dean. "Since when do you sleep so early?"

"Where'd you go for a drink, anyway?"

"Jonell's Lounge, know it?"

"Jesus! What a shithole. What kind of coworker takes you there?"

"He's from Arizona. He gets a kick out of coming down here."

"Of course. The crackheads, hookers, dope boys, hobos. It's not all like that Will Smith movie though, he should know. I never saw a bum here that looks like Will Smith," said Bud.

"I told him. He enjoys irony, like you. Right in the heart of beautiful San Francisco this refugee camp of addicts and have-nots," said Dean.

"There couldn't be a Tenderloin in Phoenix. The meth-heads would melt in the summer."

"So how's everything, Bud?"

"I haven't taken a shit in five days. We are a generation plagued by stomach problems."

Dean looked down at Bud's jelly donut and malt liquor. "You should see a doctor."

"I can't afford one on my artist's salary."

"If I told one of these corner boys what you pay for your studio, you wouldn't make it to sunrise."

"My apartment's 300 square feet and above a massage parlor."

"Your rent is more than a mortgage."

"I'm still a starving artist."

"Tuition at Academy of Art costs more than Ivy Leagues."

"Some people think you can't teach art."

"Who?"

"Not my folks," said Bud.

"If only I had your parents," said Dean.

Bud laughed and took a healthy swig. "From what I hear, you're the man with the big paycheck on the way."

"What's that mean?"

"Everyone knows."

"What do you mean by everyone?"

"How much is it?"

Dean sighed, looking around. "Ten-thousand dollars."

"Jesus! Ten stacks to move out so a museum can turn your building into its new east wing."

"I loved that apartment. So did Henriette. And I hate moving, it's no small thing."

"If I ever get in bad at the card rooms, I know whose door I'm knocking on at five in the morning."

"You're not playing again, are you?"

"I do have some willpower over temptation, you know. How do you think I live around here?"

"Just try not to tell anyone else, Henriette thinks we shouldn't."

"You were always the lucky one, Dean. Square and lucky, even back in school," said Bud.

"That's not true," said Dean.

The silver-haired woman dropped off Dean's bear claw on a warped tray that spun on the table. She went back into the kitchen. Aside from the old man sleeping near the pay phone, Dean and Bud were the only customers left.

"I've got to confess something," said Dean. He cracked open his second can. "There's a reason I called you tonight."

"It wasn't the beer and Berliners?" said Bud.

"Your jelly donut?"

"They call it a Berliner and they charge double for it, and I don't mind so long as I get to call it a Berliner."

"It wasn't the beer and Berliners."

"Talk already."

"Tonight, after I met my coworker for a drink, when I was taking my walk through the neighborhood, not even half an hour ago, I think I saw something."

"Saw something what?"

"I saw something strange." Dean leaned in. "I think I saw a prostitute get kidnapped."

Bud laughed. "What is that supposed to mean?"

"I saw a girl, she was a hooker. Definitely, I'm pretty sure. She was talking real close to this man, this creepy-looking guy, then he kind of pushed her into his minivan and drove away."

"Hookers don't get kidnapped," said Bud. "That's their job, to get into strange cars with strange men."

"But she didn't want to," said Dean.

"You know what some streetwalker wanted?"

"She looked at me. I saw her face."

"Jesus."

"She was scared. And it looked like she didn't trust this guy. It didn't seem like a pimp and hoe situation."

"Was anyone else around?"

"I was alone."

"Where?"

"Up Polk, the alley behind the old auto shop."

"Was she a tranny?"

"What difference is that?"

"She might have put up a different fight."

"She was a woman."

"How do you know?"

"I could tell."

"Famous last words."

"She looked like she wasn't from the city, maybe some place like Richmond or Vallejo. No older than twenty-one," said Dean.

"Then what happened?"

"The minivan just left."

"And you didn't do anything."

"I found something on the ground." Dean reached into his pocket and pulled out a cheap smart phone. There was a glittery Hello Kitty pendant dangling from the corner and the name *DAISY* printed in cursive on the back of the pink case.

"*Oh*," said Bud. "What's on it?"

"It's off," said Dean.

"So turn it on."

"I was thinking, maybe that's not a good idea. What if this is evidence. This girl Daisy turns up missing and I have her phone."

"You already took it and didn't go to the police."

"Should I go now?"

"You should see what's on it now."

"What if there's something weird?"

"Like what?"

"Pictures, videos—stuff you might not want to see."

"Or it's stuff you really do want to see. She is a hooker, after all."

"It might not even be her phone," said Dean. "It was lying there really conveniently."

"You're right. Someone could have planted it there, with a tracking device, one of those iPhone finders."

"Yes." Dean took a long sip of his beer and stared out at the dark and wet and windy street, a sea of black beating against the hull of their small but safe donut-transporting ship. "But *why* would someone do that?"

Bud glanced around the room. "Maybe it's some kind of scam, you're framed or blackmailed—maybe you're kidnapped, too. Maybe it's like a Japanese horror movie and whoever turns on the *pink phone* gets kidnapped and thrown into a minivan, then violated by a ghost."

Bud showed off his big, crooked grin. Dean reached for the bear claw. "I called you because you live here," said Dean. "And I thought you might have insight into this type of thing."

"The Tenderloin is my muse," said Bud.

"Then what should we do, Frida?" asked Dean.

"*I* have class at noon. So you should turn on that phone

otherwise I'm going to bed."

Too tired to argue further, Dean pressed down on the edge of the phone. The screen lit up and then settled in to a soft operational glow. It was on, like any other phone when it was on.

Dean swiped and tapped as Bud watched patiently.

"There's nothing on it," said Dean.

"There must be something."

"Not really. No Facebook, no Gmail."

"Recent calls?"

"A few received."

"Picture gallery?"

"One picture. It's her. A selfie."

Bud snatched the phone out of Dean's fingers. "She is a girl," said Bud. "Pretty, too. Too pretty to be out here."

Dean took the phone back. "Now what?"

"Now, old friend, I'm going to smoke a bowl, rub one out and go to sleep." Bud tilted his twenty-four-ounce can toward the fluorescent lights above. When it was empty, he squeezed the can just enough to put a small dent in it, stood, tightened the terrycloth belt around his waist, and zipped up his rain jacket. "How are you getting home?"

Dean sat back, dissatisfied, and closed his eyes. "My bus comes in twenty minutes. I'll start walking as soon as I finish my beer."

"I can walk you to the corner."

"I'm a big boy."

Bud grinned, amused. "I always forget. And the phone?"

"I'll call a police station tomorrow and tell them what I saw. Ask them if I should bring it in."

"Smart move."

"That's the only thing to do, right?"

"It was good seeing you, Dean. We should do this more often."

"Yes, we should."

"I mean it."

"Enjoy your class tomorrow."

"I almost forgot." Bud reached into his jacket and pulled out his old tin flask that he always carried at night. "For the road, like the old days." He tossed one back, then held it out for Dean.

"Why not." Dean took a long drink from it, then made a face. He knew it was going to be cheap whiskey but it made no difference.

"Give Henriette my regards."

"I will. Take care of yourself, Bud."

Bud started for the door. "Dean, I know I'm not much for relationship advice, but go home to Henriette already. It's probably not as bad as you think."

"Good night," said Dean.

Bud was gone and the door closed and the bell jingled loudly but the silver-haired woman did not come out of the kitchen. Dean hadn't eaten since lunch but every time he looked at the bear claw it made him nauseous. He placed his napkin over it and continued drinking.

It was only 1:15 a.m. Henriette would still be awake.

Like other guys his age he knew, Dean had often considered himself the type that would leave his girlfriend if he ever found out she was unfaithful, no matter what, but now that it really happened, to him, it didn't feel the way he thought it would. It had been a long week. The conversations, the tears, the questions. Still, he couldn't go home and see Henriette. He had nothing to say to her yet. Could a single action make you not love someone anymore? Dean once again caught himself thinking these thoughts and removed them from his head, even more effectively than the last time.

He took out the pink phone and went back to the picture gallery. The girl, Daisy, was pretty. She had dark eyes and big dimples and soft shoulders that, on their own, were able to suggest the type of body underneath, just out of frame. He thought it childish to think a thought like, *she's too beautiful to be a prostitute*, so he came to the conclusion that she was too beautiful to be a streetwalker but not too beautiful to be a stripper or high-class escort. He looked at his watch. It was over an hour ago now that he saw her. He left some cash on the table and got his wet jacket.

Outside, the rain was heavier than before and the street was emptier. Dean dug around in his jacket pocket and found a cigarette he had acquired last week with Henriette. He lit it and walked toward his bus, feeling like a nomad passing through a strange new city under the protective cover of dark. Despite the wind and rain, the walk was pleasant. But after about a block, Dean felt like resting. He decided to step down into the entrance of an old laundromat that was below street-level. He took out the pink phone from his pocket. He found the most recent received number. He went ahead and pressed it.

The phone rang. Dean crouched down low, watching the street from a different perspective, that of feeding pigeon or sewer rat. After only a few rings, a young-sounding woman answered the phone.

"Hello?" said the woman.

"Hello," said Dean.

"Who's this?"

Dean cleared his throat. "Do you know a Daisy?"

The woman laughed quietly. "Sure, I know a Daisy. Do you know a Daisy?" She had a Southern accent in her voice that he guessed she could dial up or down depending on the situation. He guessed she was dialing it up currently.

"I met her tonight," said Dean.

"She's certainly not one you forget meeting, is she?" said the woman.

"Are you a friend or relative?"

She laughed again. "You're funny. I'm a little prettier, but people sometimes confuse us for sisters."

"Did you happen to talk to Daisy tonight?"

"You tell me, sweetheart. You're calling me on her phone."

Dean put down the cigarette. "I found her phone tonight, on accident. I called to say I think your friend is in trouble."

"How do you mean?"

"I saw Daisy an hour ago. This man picked her up in a minivan, but it didn't look very consensual. I was going to go to the police but I saw your phone number and thought—"

"Was it gold?"

"Was what gold?"

"The minivan."

Dean straightened his back and looked around the street. "How did you know?"

"Don't you worry, that's just Carlos."

"Her pimp?"

"Her fiancé. And ugly as he is, that bonehead couldn't hurt a fly."

"Oh," said Dean. A car alarm went off nearby. "I guess that's a relief."

"You sound worked up."

"I was assuming the worst, I suppose."

"Maybe you watch too many movies."

"You might be right."

"Let me get this straight, you thought a kidnapper in a minivan was out rounding up hookers in the TL?" The woman laughed once more, louder this time.

"Something like that."

"Those lovebirds are always fighting."

"Fiancé or not, maybe you could check on her."

"Daisy's got three phones, I'll call her right after I'm done with you. She's a klutz, but even she can't lose three phones in one night."

"Thanks." Dean looked at his watch. He had already missed his bus. "I'm sorry for calling so late."

"It's okay, I'm sort of a night person anyway. My name is Mia. And yours?"

Dean could hear her smile through the phone. "So do you know Daisy well?" he asked.

"You could say we're colleagues," said Mia. "In fact, you could say we're both on the clock right now."

"Well, I don't mean to take more of your time," said Dean. "Maybe you could tell me where Daisy spends her time. I'd like to return the phone."

"Why don't you come to my place and give me the phone so I can give it to Daisy."

"Come to your place?"

"Sure."

"When would I do that?"

"Right now."

"I'd feel better giving her the phone myself."

"The thing is, I could tell you a million places Daisy hangs out, it doesn't mean you're going to find her."

"I guess you've got a point."

"Anyway, you sound lonely."

"I suppose everyone gets lonely sometimes."

"There's nothing wrong with being lonely."

"I know that."

"That's why you're drinking at this hour?"

"I'm not. I met a friend—two friends, earlier for drinks. I'm going home now."

"Did you think Daisy was pretty?" asked Mia. "Because you won't be disappointed when you see me."

The woman was probably lying, Dean knew, but it didn't matter. He had already matched her voice with Daisy's face.

"Come over," said Mia. "You might regret it in the morning if you don't."

"I don't think so," said Dean.

"I'll take care of you, promise."

"It's just not a good idea."

"Are you married?"

"Not yet."

"Do you have a girlfriend?"

"Not really," said Dean.

"Are you a monk?" asked Mia.

The phone beeped. Dean looked at the screen. The battery was almost dead. "I don't have a car."

"If you say you saw Daisy an hour ago, my bet's you're still in the neighborhood. I'm staying at the Pacific Hotel, past Ellis and down Jones."

"That's pretty far in there."

"Far in where?"

"It's raining, you know."

"You sound like a big boy."

"I wasn't planning to walk in that direction."

"Where were you walking?"

"Home."

"So come to my home instead," said Mia.

They both remained silent. Then Mia asked, matter-of-fact but not annoyed, "What's it going to be, sailor?"

"Okay."

"Okay, what?"

Dean stepped up onto the sidewalk and adjusted his jacket collar. "I'll start walking."

"*Lovely*," said Mia. "Fifteen minutes it is."

"Okay," said Dean.

"Wait."

"What?"

"I need to ask you a favor."

"What is it?"

"Pick me up some roses on the way?"

"Roses?"

"*Roses*, you know."

"Oh. How many roses?"

"Whatever you think's appropriate. I usually ask my clients for a dozen to fifteen for the hour."

"Okay."

"And when you get here, you need to check in at the front desk before coming up."

"Okay."

"And don't take too long, sweetheart. I need to be somewhere at three."

"Okay."

Dean ended the call. He put the pink phone back in his pocket and started walking toward Ellis Street.

Dean stopped by the ATM on Larkin. After that, he walked two blocks south, made a left on Turk, and went right on Jones. As he turned the corner, a thin man on a bicycle appeared. Dean did not notice the man, walking with his head down, trying to remember if his bank statements showed the time and location of his cash withdrawals. It made no difference, Dean knew, but he felt an odd comfort imagining it would be an interesting clue for the police if, say, he were to disappear tonight. What would Henriette think if he disappeared tonight? Now was not the time to think about her.

A police car drove past. Dean kept his eyes on his feet and walked evenly.

He crossed the street. As he did, the man on the bicycle rode over and joined Dean on the crosswalk. The man was hunched over and had one foot on his pedal, one foot floating over the pavement like a little hoverboard.

When they got to the opposite curb, the man pulled up onto it and stopped his bicycle, in front of Dean.

He cleared his throat. "Young blood," he said. "Can you spot me a ten?" His voice was coarse but gentle.

Dean looked at the man. The man got off his bike and came closer to Dean. He was tall. He looked older than Dean. His face was tired and his skin was dry. He looked too clean to be a drug addict, thought Dean, but his eyes were too focused to be totally sober. Dean told the man that he had no money.

Casually, as if pulling out a map for directions, the man took out a rock from the front pocket of his hooded sweatshirt and hit Dean, above the eyebrow, with the corner of it. Dean went down. He had never been hit with something, and as he fell, he wondered how such a small thing could be so hard. Once on the ground, Dean felt the man kick him. Then he felt the man's hands go through his pockets, back pant, front pant, outside jacket, inside jacket. There was one last kick, then it stopped.

Dean stayed still on the edge of the sidewalk. He thought he heard a woman shout something from across the street but when he opened his eyes the man on the bicycle was gone and there was nobody around. Dean crawled to the nearest wall and rested against it. His face began to turn warm as his head started to pound.

Dean felt his pockets. His keys, his wallet, the pink phone, his own phone, the $150 he had just withdrawn from the ATM, were gone. The man on the bicycle had all of Dean's personal information. He had the address to

Dean's apartment, even the keys to it.

Dean got to his feet. His socks were wet. He was dizzy. He thought he could smell freshly cut grass but there was only concrete around. Dean put his hand on the wall. He tried to walk. He wanted to go back toward Hyde. He began to move his limbs. As he did, slowly, he felt like he could start thinking clearly again. He needed to find a pay phone. All Star Donuts and Chinese Food had one, he recalled. Or perhaps Bud would still be awake. What did he say before? You always give something to the Tenderloin, Dean remembered. Yes, that's what Bud had said earlier. Dean began to hurry. He lifted his knees. He started to jog. Then Dean ran, more swiftly and efficiently than he thought he'd be able to. He had to be fast. There wasn't a lot of time. He had to call Henriette and tell her to put the deadbolt and chain on the front door.

BE SWEET AND LOVING

D ec 19 (3 days ago)

RE: Greetings from Estonia

Dear son,

Did you get my package? Are you even in Estonia still? Where is your sister? Two days ago I called Laura but nobody answered. Yesterday I emailed her. This morning I drove to their house. She would not let me in. She complained I never told her I was coming. She said my last visit stressed her out because I cleaned her house without consent! Your sister is very stubborn. Do you trust Martin, a man from Ecuador, a country plagued with drugs? Do you think he takes drugs? Laura?

Laura always accused me of loving you more but actually my love toward my two children is the same. Are you living healthy?

I dental floss my teeth nightly. I brush after meals and then use the water pick. I have cured my gingivitis. Do you keep your teeth clean?

Healthy living is important. Last week I found out the space between my toes was itchy. Now I know the best solution is not the fungus ointment, but to wash my toes twice a day and put my shoes under the sun to dry. Do you ever have rashes or itchy toes?

Please care for your body. Your Uncle John got bladder cancer. There were four tumors on his bladder. He had surgery to remove them. Smoking is one reason to get cancer. I hope you do not smoke anymore! Hair dye is the main reason for women to get bladder cancer. Will you let me buy health insurance for you?

Your father used to have dry skin when he worked at the plant. He told me too much vitamin C made his skin crack. Does that make sense to you? I suspect the chemicals damaged his skin. Please take the vitamin C I sent you. Did you receive them or not?

I believe Laura was hurt by Martin in Hawaii. Did you talk to her? I know she loves me very much but she has pushed me away since the trip. I believe Laura was injured by Martin or maybe a local criminal did something to them. It's hard to trust islander people. (Do you remember your roommate from college?) Before the trip Laura was happily asking me to cook soup for her and even thanked me twice for the good soup.

Can you video chat with her to find out her problem? Be sure she and Brie walk around in front of you. Martin reminds me of your father. Laura doesn't sound happy at all. Do you think she is safe?

When will you settle down? Can I visit you? Laura won't travel with me because I make her nervous. I really have anxiety illness. After one month sick leave, relaxation has helped me understand what's wrong with me.

Netflix was my savior. I am going to have another MRI next month and continue physical therapy. My spine doctor was very good. Can you imagine, a lot of wonderful doctors are Indian?

I am cleaning your closet now. You still have a lot of hand-some clothes. I separated them nicely. Keep up the neat order when you come to visit. Agreed?

Please try to let go of my past errors. Did you know I was also hurt deeply by my own mother and father in the past? I was happy to walk out of my parents' house and start my own life. I made a lot of mistakes. Your father was not loving at all. He had a small heart and temper. I feel so sorry for you kids to grow up with him, I hope you will forgive me. But he has his own life and you don't need to worry about him or his financial problems anymore. I live alone too, but am not lonely. Believe me, I am not lonely!

Lately I suspect people sneak into my house. One day I looked up at the book case and the Egyptian painting was missing from the frame! Last week someone moved my soup spoon. I am not senile yet, some people just enjoy playing games in the dark. Don't worry, I told the police the other day. But I have no fear. I can live with intruders.

I pray one day you and Laura can move home. I called grandpa. He agrees. I can occupy one room and the rest of the house is yours. Doesn't that sound like a deal? Or I can be your tenant and pay rent. Martin can come and go as he wishes. But if he wants me to move out, I would think Martin is very suspicious! I can cook for myself, usually I cook one meal and eat it for three days. We don't need to talk to each other unless you like to. Doesn't that sound fair?

I can help raise Brie. Did you know I started working nights when Laura was only three months old? I was a full-time mom during the day and full-time clerk at night. Laura denies my ability to take care of my own granddaughter! Have you ever heard the saying, "The older the better?" Laura must let me care for Brie otherwise my years of training are wasted!

After I retire I can move away. I will go to city college to take classes to keep me busy. I went to the senior center today. I enjoyed playing pool and the lunch conversation. People there are patient and friendly. A nice Jewish woman posted an ad looking to rent a room but she has a cat.

I am going back to work Wednesday. I may not write you as often. I must give you and Laura space to breathe.

Sometimes Laura looks peaceful with Martin. But she is always stressed with me. I think it is in my nature to be nervous and restless. Perhaps one day you can find some-one that makes life peaceful for you.

Laura is very content to be a mother. Women are by nature territorial and want to possess. No one can separate the bond between a mother and her baby. Even if you hate the world, you must love your mother. Send me more pictures.

I like your pictures.

Be sweet and loving.

Mom

p.s. Tell me if you want me to buy you health insurance!

PARK WITH POPS

The air leaves little smudges on your skin. If there's a labor law restricting how many consecutive hours you can work inside an unventilated concrete cave, Pops doesn't know about it. The air stays with you, inside your lungs, but my body is young and resilient and the money is good for someone my age. If you drive the car right up to the customer, not the designated white line, sometimes they think they're supposed to tip you. Wilfredo taught me this my first week.

I can drive stick and have no criminal record. Despite these qualifications, Pops took convincing. He distrusts anyone college-educated or thinking about becoming college-educated, and I must have given off a stench during my interview. But Pops likes me. Pops is White but most of the guys at the Park with Pops Parking Garage are a shade or two darker, Mexican or El Salvadorian or Guatemalan or Laotian or Vietnamese or Samoan or Black. We have

two brothers from Fiji. They once let me try a fish cur-
ry they made from home and laughed when I said I liked
it, eyes watery. Kahlil is a pot dealer, Dinh is a pill dealer,
Kearsey is a single dad, Fabio is a smooth talker. They call
each other names like boss, even though no one is a super-
visor. They call me kid, which I like, or sometimes professor
because I talk different, which I don't like.

The Sunday night shift is Wilfredo and me. When the
parking garage is slow, there are no cars to park or retrieve,
only the cash register to manage. You take the ticket from
the customer, enter the number, tell them how much they
owe, and they pay you. From inside the glass booth you
don't get any tips, but the air is cleaner. There are worse
things you could be doing for a buck, Wilfredo always says,
toothpick hanging. I believe Wilfredo has an old soul, and
when he shares his wisdom people seem to listen. Maybe it's
his healthy beard or his calming baritone.

My grandmother is happy about my new job. Since
we came to live with her, she tells me and my brother that
we've become too soft. She worked nights at the post office
for twenty-eight years. What did we ever do to deserve
to grow up in a safe neighborhood with decent schools?
We don't know, we always tell her. Grandma tells us that
spending time around working-class men, like our grandpa
was, is important.

To pass the time, Wilfredo asks a lot of questions. He
asks if I've ever been with a girl and I answer yes, which

is a lie. He asks if I've ever been in a fight, and I say once, another lie. He asks what I plan to do after high school and I say I don't know. Wilfredo asks if I'm lying. But normally I tell him the truth and he seems to tell me the truth, like when he tells me the story of how he slept with this stripper he met in Centerfolds last Labor Day weekend while his girlfriend was out of town.

When business is really slow, Wilfredo parks his Cadillac next to the glass booth and we sit inside and watch Cheech and Chong on a video screen on his dashboard. He's saving up to buy an '84 Coupe de Ville and when I ask him what's wrong with the Cadillac he has now, he tells me that the car he has now, what we're sitting in, is an Oldsmobile.

That summer, Wilfredo teaches me a lot of useful things like how to tell if Pops is in a bad mood or how to bribe Kearsey into punching your timecard for you when you're late—a bag of sunflower seeds. But Wilfredo also teaches me more important things like how to roll a joint, how to tell if a girl wants to go home with you, and how to not let your surroundings define you. Wilfredo grew up on the east side of town to poor parents with gang affiliations and prides himself on having an honest job and loving family he can take care of.

On a hot night in August, Wilfredo is late and when he arrives, there is blood on the soft top of his car. He tells me that his cousin was shot in front of him, outside his house. But he says I shouldn't worry, it's not a problem and nobody knows where he works. Wilfredo is a little quieter than usual and the whole night I wonder if he is angry or sad or just tired. He eventually tells me about how terrible his dad was and how he will be different for his son. He says that he is stealing money from the register and that one day he will open his own car rental company. He tells me that I'm too smart to work at a dump like this. He says that Pops has a hot wife.

The next Sunday is my last day. I bring a gift for Wilfredo, a metal bottle opener with a little Cadillac logo on it. But when I show up, there is only Pops and a police officer. "Wilfredo was shot last night but is doing okay now," says Pops. I answer a few questions from the officer, then I finish my shift. At the end of the night, I thank Pops for the opportunity and we shake hands. I give him the bottle opener and ask Pops to give it to Wilfredo whenever he returns.

My summer job ends.

That fall, I move to San Diego. It takes time to adjust to college life, they tell me. I study business. I ride a bicycle to class. The campus is really beautiful. Sometimes they shoot movies on it. My roommate is from the O.C., like the TV show. Here, there are 320 sunny days a year, crime is lower than in most Southern California cities, and when the sky is clear and wind is strong, you can feel the ocean in the air right on your skin.

RHUBARB PIE

The walls of her cubicle are low. Barbara sits at her desk, her cornmeal oxford shirt crinkled and untucked at her hips, her white athletic socks showing, her curly black hair flattened on one side, glinting with the kind of rich human shine you only get from not showering three or more days. Sometimes I'm reminded of *Fight Club* when I look at my coworker, but I know that Barbara isn't the leader of an underground bare-knuckle boxing organization. That's artisanal jam on her shirt collar, not blood.

"The Guzo report, I need it before our 10 a.m.," says Kip, finger-drumming his pack of Gauloises Blondes.

"I left two copies on your desk," says Barbara.

"That was last week, dumb dumb. Aren't you analysts supposed to be good at counting?"

Barbara turns red. Kip proceeds, off toward the elevators, toward his morning smoke, toward his morning dump. Barbara pointed this whole routine out to me one morning last December and now I notice it even when I don't want to.

According to her business card, Barbara is Junior Business Analyst at the Applebum Group. But that's not what she really is. Barbara is a pastry chef. A damn good one, if I can say so. Cakes and puff pastries come easiest for her but fruit pies and tarts are her passion. She goes to culinary school during the evenings on Tuesdays and Fridays and helps with catering gigs on the weekend when she is lucky. Once, after a few rounds of margaritas, Barbara told me that on her last day at the Applebum Group—which will be the same day she tells the company she's leaving—she plans to throw her best and most beloved dessert of all time, key lime pie, right in the face of Kip Applebum.

That day is today.

I've worked at the Applebum Group for seven years, five more than Barbara. I have the same title I had when I started, my salary has increased at one percent each year, and I get ten days of annual vacation. But I get health insurance and a gift card to the Olive Garden every Christmas. I hate working at the Applebum Group the same as Barbara. The difference between us is that I appear to like it, which goes a long way. I tuck in my shirt, take regular showers, and even get along with Kip Applebum (don't let the last name fool you, he married into the family and changed *his* last name). But the most important difference between

Barbara and myself is this: Barbara is a talented, passionate, red-blooded pastry chef, and I am a mediocre writer at best, who has spent more years of his life talking about writing than actually writing.

I need the Applebum Group. People like Barbara, they never do.

After her 10 a.m. meeting, Barbara meets me in the Curiosity breakroom. There's no coffee maker and the freezer smells, making it a good place for offline conversation. I greet her with a congratulatory fist bump when she walks in.

"All good things," I say.

"I'm not at the finish line yet," says Barbara.

"Does Kip know already?"

"That I'm throwing a pie at him today?"

"That today is your last day."

"I get my final paycheck at four-thirty, the timing for it couldn't be better."

"Barbara, you're not really going to do this."

"I've been up all night!"

"Key lime pie doesn't take all night. Even I know that."

"But you see, I didn't make key lime pie."

"Or lemon meringue."

"I've got to show you something." Barbara opens the refrigerator door and, as if sliding back a tray of marbles, reveals a beautiful, glowing, billboard-worthy pie, strips of brushed golden dough crisscrossed atop a mysteriously molten red filling.

"Are those raspberries?" I ask.

"Rhubarb."

"You baked a rhubarb pie to throw in Kip Applebum's face?"

"Not so loud," whispers Barbara as she pokes her head in the hallway.

"That doesn't make sense—the whole point of throwing a key lime pie is that it's fluffy, like in cartoons! A rhubarb pie is dense and lumpy and seems hard to throw. Why didn't you just bake a calzone?"

"Rhubarb is tart. Like our experiences working at the Applebum Group—mine, at least."

"Fine, I get it."

"Also, I was in a meeting once presenting to Regional and some of the real Applebums when, right as I put up a red pie chart slide, Kip took out that stupid little Sharper Image laser pointer of his and— "

"I remember," I say.

"No one could stop laughing for the rest of the meeting," says Barbara.

"It was an hour meeting, too."

"Look, friend, I have to ask a favor."

"Barbara, I think you're making a mistake. But I told you before, I won't stop you."

"I need you to help me."

"Help you what?"

"I need you to help me pie Kip."

"Are you kidding?"

"There's nobody else."

"No."

"Please."

"No way in hell."

"I'm asking you, buddy——"

"I said no, Barbara."

"You said it yourself! You can't stand the place."

"Well, we can't all frolic around all day like we've got nothing to lose," I declare. "We're not all pastry chefs, for Christ's sake."

Barbara folds the tin foil back over her creation.

"You're right," says Barbara, crimping the edge closest to her. "Just forget I asked."

My quarterly team lunch at Red Lobster ends early and afterward I find myself still irritated at Barbara's ridiculous request and her belief that I'd say yes. After all, I still have a career at the Applebum Group, LinkedIn connections I need to maintain for my future. But oddly enough, I soon fantasize about not only helping Barbara throw the rhubarb pie, but about hurling the rhubarb pie—make that the key lime pie—myself, and then shouting, "Eat shit and die, Applebum! I *QUIT!*" as I march toward the elevator and along the way kiss Tatiana, our receptionist, for good measure.

That would be one hell of a story. A story I could actually write. In fact, as I continue to imagine the expression on Kip's face and the roar of the office behind me, I start to scribble parts of the story down, right on a sheet of computer paper. It's been a long time since I wrote like this, without trying, and it feels good. I write off and on for the rest of the afternoon and ignore my emails.

Just after 4 p.m., I meet Barbara again, this time in the Collaboration breakroom because we both need coffee. We fill our mugs and tap creamer dust from the can without speaking.

Finally, I ask, "Since when does one pie take two people to throw?"

Barbara holds back her smile and finds me a stirrer. "Kip leaves every day at five, as you know. I wanted to catch him then, on his way out, but it occurred to me—I have to pie Kip inside the office. In front of everyone."

"That makes sense."

"I want you to know, I'm throwing this pie alone. It's just me, myself and pie."

"So then?"

"I need you to schedule an emergency meeting with Kip at 4:45 inside the Synergy meeting room," says Barbara. "Then as soon as he steps out—splat."

"Synergy, across from the courtyard?"

"Fast getaway."

"Won't they stop you in the parking lot?"

"I didn't drive today, I'm going to run all the way home."

"Faster getaway."

"Look, I even wore my cute New Balances."

"Kip will suspect I was a part of this."

"I thought about that," says Barbara. "You've got a good thing going here. I need your help, let's be clear, but I'd feel like a real asshole if I were the one to muck things up for you."

"Don't lose sleep over it."

"I'm serious. You don't have to do this."

"Kip Applebum deserves to be pied. I admire what you're doing, Barbara. I really do."

"What are you saying?"

"You were never supposed to work at the Applebum Group in the first place," I say as I open the Outlook calendar on my phone. "Let's send you off right, pastry chef."

Witnesses would tell me months later that while it was a respectable throw on Barbara's behalf, the rhubarb pie landed mostly in Kip's ear and shirt collar. I do remember hearing the splat, sitting nervously in the Synergy room after my bogus meeting with Kip, and thinking that it didn't sound like a splat so much as a thwack. Witnesses would also tell me that the rhubarb pie didn't really explode, at least, not the way the key lime pie with whipped cream did in my adaptation of the story, it just sort of crumbled upon impact, sliding off in tectonic slabs, falling slowly to the hallway carpet. I guess it was all the same to Barbara.

When I finally came out, I saw a reasonable mess, nothing too bad, just a spill that would take a few minutes to clean. I watched Barbara sprint through the courtyard toward the setting afternoon sun; I had never seen the woman run so fast. In the weeks to follow, Kip never brought up the rhubarb pie to me or building security or anyone for that matter, understandably.

That June, I left the Applebum Group.

LIKE A CHAMPION

On the old corkboard near the Bowser Hog Island streetcar was the list of things Georgie wanted to do before the week ended and the shop closed forever. Uncle Jen made lists. Georgie left them up on the walls of this place. *Outstanding Bills. Kids Who Stole Stuff.* Georgie titled his list *Like a Champion Last Acts* and written neatly at the top of the list were things like *Find Nice Homes for Remaining Inventory (incl. Rocket Firing Boba Fett), Give Thank You Beanie Babies to Friends of Shop, Mail Udo Final Paycheck with Valor Bonus (as Promised!)*, and in slightly smaller, harder to read letters, *Ask Out FedEx Lady Before Big Regret.*

"Ten percent? Hell kind of closing sale is this?"

This town. Sometimes Georgie wondered what they put in the water. Cheapskate juice? Goober concentrate? Georgie got off the train-watching stool and went out to the front room.

"Good eye, very rare that one," said Georgie.

The man in the suit jacket and dark jeans looked up and gave the Lance Armstrong Tour de France bobblehead back to his boy.

"You went to my high school," said the man. "Sure, Little Georgina and his Uncle Jenny! How is the crusty old tool?"

Georgie felt his face turn warm but kept a pleasant smile. "Ten percent is a superb discount for that item. If it's not to your liking, perhaps I can recommend the PennyMart down the street?"

"Come on son, we're late." The man bleeped his car outside. "Remember what I told you about why school was so important?"

The door closed and the shop was quiet again. Monday morning customers were the worst, Uncle Jen used to say. Georgie just didn't like running into old jerks from school. He could tell right when someone walked in if they were from this town or not. Take the FedEx Lady. She was kind and lovely and respectful, definitely not from this place. Was she too lovely? Did Georgie have no chance?

Georgie switched on the NASCAR Victory Lane race car track by the window. Well, FedEx Lady was very pretty, but not on some gold pedestal or something, was she? Sure, she was elegant but also a bit stout, probably from all the lifting, and her face was sweet as pie but those bags under her eyes. She was no spring chicken. Just like Georgie. Oh lord, had he lost it? Had he looked in a mirror? Georgie would be so lucky if a girl like FedEx Lady looked twice at him! He was no dream boat. His body was skinny and fat lately, depending where you looked, his hair was starting to thin in front, and his neck mole. When it was warm, a hair grew out of it.

At least his face was symmetrical. Georgie read once in a science magazine that women, genetically speaking, cared most about face symmetry. More than muscles or hair or personality or nice suit jackets.

Anyway, Uncle Jen was the ladies man of the shop. Maybe that contributed to his stroke. Too much hay-rolling in his younger days. It had been a while since Georgie rolled in hay.

The door jingled and the Lima Boy walked in.

"Shouldn't you be in school?" asked Georgie as he climbed the ladder and began rearranging the *Alien* and *Predator* figures, first by film, then height. They would have to sell this week.

"How much for this one, Georgie?" asked the Lima Boy from the comic book stacks.

"Katsuhiro Otomo is twenty-five."

"*Twenty-five?* Oh man, you know I don't have no job."

"Buddy, I was about your age when I started working here every day after school. Time to use that noggin and start thinking about what you want to do when you grow up."

The Lima Boy shrugged. "What will you do once the

shop closes?"

Georgie stopped rearranging. "I'll be sad for a while, sure. That's life. But don't worry about me. Maybe I'll come back next year with an even bigger, better shop. One that would really make Uncle Jen proud. What do you think of that?"

The Lima Boy inhaled loudly like he was preparing to dive to the bottom of a pool, then he spun suddenly and darted out the door with a thick, glossy Japanese graphic novel under his arm.

"You son of a bitch!" Georgie leapt off the ladder.

He ran as fast he could after the kid, out the shop and all the way down Fundy Lane, but somewhere along Biscay Lane he lost him. The little shrimp was fast. Some shoppers outside the PennyMart across the street started laughing but Georgie was too winded to care. His knee hurt and his shoelace had come untied.

As Georgie limped back to the shop, he imagined what he would do to the kid. Hold him down and shave him bald. Make him scrub the shop windows wearing a sign that read *CROOK*. No, that wasn't right. The Lima Boy was just a child. How come his parents didn't give him enough money for comic books?

The twerp did have a good question though. What was Georgie going to do once the shop closed? He had spent more time in that shop than anywhere else on this planet, and more time with Uncle Jen than anyone. Opening a new shop was pure fantasy. It would take years and who's to say it wouldn't also go down in flames? Uncle Jen would turn over in his grave. If only he were still around. Uncle Jen always gave Georgie sound life advice. Then again, Uncle Jen died alone with no kids or girlfriend or money and actually had lots of debt and a car that didn't even go in reverse. All he had in this world was the shop and his late sister's son and Georgie was out buying Funyuns that afternoon when the stroke happened and Uncle Jen collapsed in the backroom in his cargo shorts and simply stopped breathing. Did Georgie want to end up like that?

He walked past the Family Time Beer and Liquor store and PhoNomenal Vietnamese restaurant. Like a Champion. An entire store celebrating winners and heroes and warriors. And what the hell was Georgie, the guy inside? Had he ever done anything in his life that was heroic or brave or meaningful?

When Georgie got back to the shop, the door was still open. The FedEx Lady was inside.

Oh, boy. FedEx Lady's brown ponytail twisted out playfully through her cap and her knee-length blue shorts revealed legs that were tanned and perhaps a tad thick, but tapered down handsomely into tasteful work boots. Not that he was ogling, just noticing. He would also notice if a guy was standing there like that, though he guessed that would be suspicious if he was staring at another man's calves so long but again he wasn't staring, just noticing.

FedEx Lady turned around. "Georgie, I know you want to get rid of your stuff, but you can't just leave your door open for the world."

"I know. That damn Lima Boy, I chased him halfway to the water park."

FedEx Lady saw the sweat on Georgie's forehead. "I'm sure you scared the little shit good. Your boxes are by the backroom, just need the old signature as usual."

Georgie went around the counter and got his pen. When he finished signing, he asked, "Would you like a Beanie Baby?"

"A Beanie what?" asked FedEx Lady.

Georgie opened the glass and got Icy, the fluffy white seal with hopeful eyes. "They were big in the nineties. Can still be pretty valuable. There was once a Princess Diana Beanie Baby that sold for three hundred grand, can you believe that?"

"No kidding?" FedEx Lady examined the Beanie Baby curiously then placed it carefully into her messenger pouch. "That's certainly a lot of money."

"Oh, one more thing." Georgie took out an envelope and handed it to FedEx Lady.

"Overnight express?"

"IRS forms."

"The neighborhood won't be the same without you, Georgie. You're one of the good ones," said FedEx Lady.

Georgie watched her as she wrote. "Say, would you like

to go out sometime? I don't know if Federal Express allows that sort of thing, fraternizing with clients, but there's a coffee place that opened nearby and it's getting pretty good reviews on Yelp."

FedEx Lady put down her clipboard. "That's sweet of you, Georgie. Really. But it's kind of hard to have coffee breaks the way we work, with the time schedule and gas and traffic conditions, plus I'm already on probation."

"Of course, traffic conditions."

"So how about dinner instead?"

"At a restaurant?"

"If you're paying. I'm a little low on funds this month." She laughed sadly then looked at her watch. "Crap, I'm running late again. Mills is going to fire my ass."

"How about Wednesday night?"

"You don't waste time, do you Georgie?"

"I know a place that does something special Wednesdays."

"Okay, then."

"Should we meet here at seven?"

"Why not, I don't have my night classes this week," said FedEx Lady. "Aren't you forgetting something?"

"Do you have food allergies?" asked Georgie.

"My name, Einstein. It's Felicia, in case you were ever planning to ask." Felicia smiled and when she did, her eyes squinted like she was looking into the sun or something else bright and that made Georgie feel warm inside and he began to sweat again as he returned a smile of his own. Felicia left the shop and jumped gracefully into her truck.

Felicia the FedEx Lady.

The door closed and two old timers came in. Georgie said hello then excused himself and went into the backroom to the lists on the walls and wrote *Lima Boy* on the list above the broken microwave and *Done!* on the list on the old corkboard. When he came back out, the old timers were gone.

Every Tuesday, Georgie had lunch with the Association of Successful Small Business Owners, ASSBO, at the Round Table Pizza on Hudson Lane. They sat outside on the sidewalk and watched people walk by like Italians do in Italy. Georgie had never been but Mr. Cadbury had been twice during his service days. There was Mr. Cadbury of Caddy's Used Golf Club Shack, Miss Wong of Wong Way Travel and Holiday, and Gustavo of The 99 Cent Store. The big news of the day was the cat burglar in town.

"All my putters, a wedge and get this—the Big Bertha hanging from the ceiling! This wasn't your normal two-bit knucklehead, this guy knew his golf clubs," said Mr. Cadbury before finishing his Hefeweizen and biting into the soaked orange slice. Citrus squirted onto his white mustache.

"Oh, it's terrible! The thief took my little airplane models and that Pan Am stewardess mannequin in my window. I'm going to miss Veronica." Miss Wong shook her head with sorrow as she added parmesan to her pizza.

Georgie always found that mannequin creepy and a bit unnecessary for a travel agency, but he consoled Miss Wong with a slice of his Wombo Combo. She always ate when she was stressed.

"What a sick nut," said Gustavo, flipping down the sun clips on his glasses. "One can only imagine what is happening to Veronica as we speak."

Miss Wong squealed in horror then took another bite.

"I can only speculate as no one has ever robbed The 99 Cent Store," said Gustavo. "But I think it's an inside job."

"Meaning what exactly?" asked Georgie.

"The government! Those politicians are always playing golf and they've got their hands deep in the pockets of the airlines. Plenty of incentive to take down a local travel tycoon."

"Thanks for calling me a tycoon," said Miss Wong.

"You don't know what the hell you're talking about, Gus," said Mr. Cadbury. "There ain't no conspiracy. When the economy goes downhill, people steal. Plain and simple. And this town is going to shit!"

The uninterested teenage waiter returned with a fresh Hefeweizen for Mr. Cadbury and ranch dressing for Gustavo.

"So how come nobody stole from Georgie?" asked Gustavo.

"Because this town remembers Uncle Jen, that's why.

They know that's one shop not to fuck with. If the world knew it was only little Georgie here running the place, they'd knock it over in a heartbeat." Mr. Cadbury pounded his fist on the table then raised his beer glass. "To Uncle Jen! A good man!"

Georgie raised his Fanta. "Once, Uncle Jen found a raccoon stealing out of the storage shed behind the shop. He threw the poor guy over the Ramirez fence."

"Raccoon versus pitbull," said Gustavo nodding, imagining the match up.

"Hey, kid," said Mr. Cadbury. "You did your best with the shop. Don't let nobody tell you differently. Running a successful small business takes grit, backbone. It ain't for everyone."

"What is that supposed to mean?" asked Georgie.

"I just hope this burglar is done with us," said Miss Wong, twisting her napkin into a little churro. "I can't live in fear like this."

"We'll watch out for one another," said Georgie.

"I don't need watching out," said Mr. Cadbury. "If I catch the punk, he's getting a nine iron up the ass."

"If he's a he," said Miss Wong.

"I know one thing," said Gustavo as he emptied his ranch over his Maui Zaui. "I'm going to start locking up my shop extra carefully at night, maybe rig trip wires around the premises. Shoot, I might get a pitbull myself."

The waiter returned, untroubled by the crime wave.

"Something else I can get you fine businessmen and businesswomen?"

"Screw it, cinnamon twists," said Miss Wong.

"More ranch," said Gustavo.

"Another Hef," said Mr. Cadbury.

"Make that two," said Georgie.

"Well, Georgie, I hate to bring up the elephant on the patio," said Mr. Cadbury. "But seeing as this is your last week as a successful small business owner, on behalf of the association, I'd like to say thank you for your industry insights this past year and I guess this means goodbye. Not goodbye forever, of course, just goodbye until you own a successful small business again."

Miss Wong looked down. "Sorry, Georgie. We've all agreed to pay for your lunch."

"Yeah, anything you want pal, so long as it's under thirty dollars," added Gustavo.

Mr. Cadbury finished his fourth Hefeweizen and bit into his orange slice again. Citrus squirted across the table.

When Georgie got back to the shop, a group of high school kids were out front smoking pot. He could smell the stuff two stores down. The nerve. He ran toward the teenagers angrily and waved them away, like they were a pack of pigeons, and they jumped up laughing and screaming before escaping across the street with their skateboards. They chucked their soda cans at Georgie. One was full. Maybe this town was going to shit. Georgie picked up the cans and went inside to change his shirt.

That afternoon, the retail gods were smiling down on Georgie. Like a Champion sold forty-seven items in total. Some were only Pokémon cards and Lego sets, but he also found homes for his Mike Tyson '82 Junior Olympics action figure and original-release Tickle Me Elmo. It wasn't enough to retire to the Bahamas, but every sale helped. Satisfied, Georgie packed up a few minutes early and put away the shop's most valuable items in his secret hiding place in the backroom. Before leaving, Georgie also took out the trash, broke down the old shelves near the entrance, left a message for Udo asking if he received his final paycheck, and called the restaurant to make his reservation for Felicia and him the following evening. He jiggled every lock twice then closed up for the night.

It was a productive day.

That night, Georgie watched old episodes of *Star Trek*. Afterward, he had a dream about Felicia. Georgie was the captain of a spaceship and Felicia was his co-captain. They were headed to a new planet to rebuild the human race or something. They were chosen by an alien planning committee because they were ideal humans, not only because of Felicia's legs and Georgie's face symmetry, but because they both knew a lot about surviving and what it meant to be human. Felicia knew about making ends meet with an evil boss like Mills breathing down her neck. And Georgie, with his mother dying young and single uncle raising him, knew about independence and hard work. Sometimes it was damn lonely spending his days in the shop and not out looking for love like most humans, but the aliens respected that about him. He was selfless. Somewhere over the Milky Way, Felicia and Georgie floated toward each other and kissed. Wow, she was a really good kisser in zero gravity. But once they landed, the spaceship turned into a Hometown Buffet that Georgie vaguely remembered from his childhood, and it wasn't Felicia but wrinkly old Mr. Hartkinson from the leather shoe repair store suddenly in front of him.

Georgie woke cold and alone. He thought about Felicia some more and then fell back asleep.

Wednesday morning started like any other. It wasn't until about an hour passed that Georgie realized Like a Champion had been robbed. There were no papers on the floor or tall cabinets tipped over like in the movies. Everything was exactly the same except for one thing. All the Beanie Babies were missing.

Georgie gave his information to the police and by lunchtime the shop re-opened. He wanted to call the members of ASSBO to tell them he too had been robbed, but he didn't want to alarm them. This would be quite a blow to his closing sale. After all, his Beanie Baby collection could probably sell for more than a thousand bucks. Well, at least the cat burglar didn't find Boba Fett.

The Boba Fett with Rocket Firing Jetpack action figure

was released by Kenner in 1979, a mail-in promotion for *The Empire Strikes Back*. After reports of children choking and going blind from the spring-loaded rocket, Kenner recalled the toy, making it very hard to find these days. Boba was the most valuable item in the shop. Even in its non-mint condition, it could go for five, maybe ten thousand dollars. Uncle Jen once suggested selling it on eBay but Georgie refused and Uncle Jen never asked again. That wasn't what collecting was about. Georgie loved seeing the joy on someone's face the moment they bought something that was rare and special to them. He would never get to see that now with the Beanie Babies.

All afternoon, Georgie thought about the Beanie Babies. Why would the burglar steal only Beanie Babies? Why nothing else? It would require someone with insider knowledge about collectibles. Or someone with no knowledge about collectibles. Georgie went through flimsy suspect after flimsy suspect, from the Lima Boy to the newspaper delivery fellow to the weird scarf lady that came in Sundays and never bought anything. Nothing made much sense.

There was only one name that kept floating to the top of his list no matter how many times he pushed it down.

Felicia.

Was it possible? It seemed like a far-fetched theory, but maybe it wasn't. Felicia was the only friend of the shop to whom Georgie had given a Beanie Baby, and one of only a few people in town who knew anything about what Beanie Babies could be worth. Perhaps her FedEx job was just a ruse to get her inside every shop in town. Maybe she used her truck to transport the stolen merchandise. Was poor Veronica in that truck? Big Bertha? Even though Georgie wasn't a member of the ASSBO anymore, those guys were good people and his friends, and he had a sick feeling in his stomach thinking that he might know the person responsible for robbing them. Maybe Mr. Cadbury was right. When the economy went downhill, people stole. Maybe even people who normally wouldn't do such a thing.

Hold on, thought Georgie. Come on. This was preposterous, wasn't it? There was no way the cat burglar was really Felicia.

But if it wasn't Felicia, thought Georgie, who the hell else could have stolen the Beanie Babies? Georgie had no answers.

Before he knew it, Georgie started to feel angry and confused and betrayed as a stream of reasonable and unreasonable questions filled his head. It eventually led to one last one. Did Felicia really want to go on this date with Georgie or was it all part of some elaborate plan to steal from him again?

What a cruel world. Georgie had finally gotten a date with a wonderful girl, and here she was a heartless petty criminal. Well, thought Georgie, he had an opportunity soon to find out for sure.

Before the date, Georgie meditated in the back room, watching the Bowser Hog Island streetcar go round and round on the track, chugging past the central station, the sweetgum trees, the tiny neighborhood milkman.

Georgie changed into his clean sneakers and put on a collared shirt. He rubbed Uncle Jen's old LA Looks styling gel into his hair. Then Georgie reached down into his secret hiding place, the plastic Batcave Command Center playset beneath the train table, and retrieved Boba Fett. Boba was going to be seen tonight.

Out in the front room, Georgie placed Boba Fett inside a large glass display box right on the main counter, visible for the whole neighborhood to see. The box had LED lights around the edges and when Georgie plugged the thing in, Boba Fett standing there in the center of it, it lit up like a modern art display. It was perfect. Then Georgie placed the Family Protect Teddy Bear Nanny Cam next to the Aliens eleven-inch Sigourney Weaver action figure up on the top shelf. He pointed the teddy bear's camera, its round brown eyes, down at the glass display box. Georgie turned out the shop lights and locked the front door. He left the windows open.

Georgie waited outside for Felicia. A shiny SUV soon arrived and pulled into a parking spot nearby. The door opened and Felicia got out. Georgie began to sweat again.

Felicia wore a yellow summer dress and as she made her way down the sidewalk, the setting sun created a soft glow around her shapely body. She was stunning. Without her blue cap and uniform, she looked so different. She was definitely too lovely for Georgie. She was definitely on a gold pedestal and it was big and twenty-four karats. Georgie got nervous. When they hugged hello, Georgie suddenly wanted to smell her and hold her and tell her he loved her and that he had been waiting for someone like her his entire life. But Georgie forced himself to relax. He told himself to stick to his plan.

It was still warm out, so Georgie and Felicia walked to the restaurant. As they passed through the main square, they both agreed it was a pleasant evening and that sometimes this town wasn't so bad.

Felicia laughed when they got to the restaurant.

"I didn't know Applebee's had All-You-Can-Eat Boneless Wing Wednesdays," she said. They walked past the fun window art and into the busy establishment.

The reservation worked and they were seated at a booth near the corner of the bar.

"Is the place okay?" asked Georgie.

"Honestly, I love places like this," said Felicia. "They're cheesy and silly and you know what? Anyone too cool for Applebee's is too cool for me."

"I'm glad." Georgie smiled. "My uncle used to take me here. Our record was fifty-eight wings."

"They really don't stop you?"

"You just have to finish in two hours."

"I'm sorry about your uncle by the way, I don't think I ever got the chance to tell you that."

"He had a bad ticker. I just wish I could have kept his shop afloat a little while longer for him."

"Well, you outlasted the KB Toys. The internet will eventually conquer all. Your uncle would be proud of everything you did in this economic landscape."

An elderly waiter came and politely took their order before slipping away to the kitchen.

"Do you have any family in town?" asked Georgie.

"My mom's still around. Actually she lives with me. Don't run! It's not as bad as it sounds. She got sick a few years ago and I decided to move to a bigger place with an extra bedroom. FedEx has great benefits so it worked out with hospital bills and stuff."

"That's amazing that you do that."

"It sounds more noble than it is. She gets on my nerves and I fight with her pretty much everyday."

"I don't want to see your bad side."

"No, you don't." Felicia winked.

The waiter carefully served the first round of wings and beers, then did a sort of bow and left.

"You said you take night classes?" asked Georgie.

"Supply chain management," said Felicia. "Very unexciting. But it's a good fit for my career at FedEx, after a few years maybe I can oversee a whole operation somewhere. But my professor got food poisoning this week." Felicia picked up a neon orange wing.

"Sounds like a hell of a plan," said Georgie.

"Have you ever thought about going back to school?"

"Me? No way, I was never any good at it. I've got an okay memory about stuff I like, I just didn't like what they taught in school."

"Since you'll be unemployed soon, maybe I can help." Felicia furrowed her brows. "I can imagine you as some pop culture historian, a sports writer, a toy designer! You're old school. You could teach one of these corporations how to make toys with soul, how they used to."

Georgie laughed. She was funny. Then Georgie said, "Or maybe I could become a master thief."

Felicia put down her wing and looked at Georgie. "A thief? You? Now that I can't imagine. You've got to be nimble to be a thief. Hell Georgie, you couldn't even catch the Lima Boy."

"I think that kid was on something."

Felicia laughed then fiddled with her beer bottle label. "Georgie, I've got to confess something."

"Please." Georgie sat up straight, ready.

"Here goes," said Felicia. "I'm sort of coming off a bad break up. This is actually the first date I've had in a while. I think you're a nice guy, not like the normal jerks I date, so I'm optimistic. But I just want to take things slow."

"Oh. Of course."

Her phone vibrated. Felicia looked at the screen.

"Sorry, I need to take this." She stood and went toward the bathrooms. Georgie caught himself noticing her nice legs again as she walked away.

Oh, what the hell was Georgie doing! This wasn't the plan at all. Georgie finished his beer. The date was going too well. He was being too nice. Felicia was being too lovely, that's why. Perhaps she was playing him for a fool. He should stick to the plan. He would stick to the plan. He was going to ask her the hard questions when she returned.

Felicia sat back down just as the waiter came with the next round of wings and beers.

"What'd I miss?" asked Felicia.

"How'd you like that Beanie Baby I gave you?" asked Georgie.

Felicia paused. "Oh, that cute little seal thing? I love it!"

"Where did you end up putting it, may I ask?"

"I think by my bed somewhere." Felicia looked up, thinking. "Yes, in that general vicinity."

"Those Beanie Babies can be worth a lot, you know."

"I remember you telling me. I sure hope the one you gave me wasn't worth a lot."

"Do you know Mr. Cadbury from the used golf shop?"

"Why?"

"His place got robbed this week."

"That's awful. You know, some of our drivers have been getting robbed too, right out of the back of their trucks."

"You don't say. Felicia, where were you last night?"

"Excuse me?"

"I'm just curious, what were you doing?"

"I like you Georgie, but to be honest, I'm not quite sure that's any of your business." Felicia smiled politely, not yet upset.

"I was home watching *Star Trek*," said Georgie.

"Okay, if you must know, I was also home. Playing Connect Four with my mother, I'm embarrassed to say."

"From what time to what time?"

"Is something the matter, Georgie?"

"Who called your phone just now?"

"Excuse me?" Felicia was upset this time.

Georgie played with one of the bare chicken bones. "Want to know what the most valuable item in my shop is? It's this Boba Fett action figure from the seventies. If someone wanted to, if they were patient, found the right buyer, they could probably sell it for ten thousand dollars."

"What is a Boba Fett?"

"Ten thousand dollars is a lot of money."

"Look, I think I know what this is about. Don't freak out about your shop, Georgie. It's just a toy store, after all. You've got to keep things in perspective. You'll be back on your feet in no time."

"You know what, Felicia? Actually, I'm not feeling very well. I think I'm sick. I need to go home and rest."

"You're sick?"

"I'm not feeling well, I think I may even stay home

tomorrow. If you're looking for me, I'll be at home sick in my bed. I definitely won't be at the shop."

"Okay." Felicia was confused. "Would you like me to walk you home?"

"Don't worry about me, just go back to your car by the shop. I'll be fine by myself at home." Georgie stood and placed cash on the table.

"I'm not sure what happened," said Felicia, also rising. "But I think there's been some kind of misunderstanding."

"Well, we'll have to sort it out another day." Georgie looked at Felicia as she simply stared back, waiting for some kind of explanation.

"Feel better then," said Felicia.

Georgie left Felicia alone at the table and walked out of the still-busy restaurant without looking back.

When Georgie got home, he went straight to bed. He fell asleep a few hours later.

Georgie had a dream about Uncle Jen. Georgie was the quarterback of the New York Jets and it was the Super Bowl. Uncle Jen was the coach, yelling at Georgie from the sidelines, jumping up and down in his cargo shorts and brown leather jacket, his stringy hair poking out from a Vince Lombardi hat. Every time Georgie got the football he only threw ducks, too short or too long or straight up in the air. The crowd booed. Uncle Jen would yell. *"Get your head in the game! You're a good kid Georgie, but sometimes you can be a real dumbass! Stubborn and blind and a real dumbass! Always have been! Open your damn eyes Georgie and stop being a dumbass!"* Georgie got the ball again and a lineman squashed him. Georgie lay on his back staring at the pale sky when Uncle Jen appeared, face big as the moon, looking older and weaker then Georgie remembered. He glared down and yelled. *"Don't be like me, idiot! I had a terrible life. Can't you see that? Didn't you ever open your eyes? I had a terrible life! Dumbass! Now get up and win for once!"* Georgie stood and the crowd cheered and the cheerleaders danced but Georgie didn't feel like playing football anymore.

When he woke, his bedroom was already bright. Georgie got dressed. He left his apartment without eating breakfast and hurried down to the shop.

When Georgie opened the shop that Thursday morning, all of his suspicions were confirmed. The Boba Fett was missing. The glass display on the counter was still plugged in and the LED lights were still on, but the box was completely empty. Georgie climbed the ladder to the top shelf and got the Family Protect Teddy Bear Nanny Cam he had put there the day before. He took it with him into the backroom.

As Georgie hunched over the black-and-white TV monitor and started the video footage from the plugged-in teddy bear, he tried to prepare himself for the consequences of this evidence. Would he really go to the police if Felicia was on the tape? What would he say to her? Would he ask for Boba Fett back? He watched the monitor for a long time, seeing only car headlights pass in and out of frame.

Then a short figure with long hair entered the shop, right through the front door. Georgie squinted and moved his face close to the video monitor. The recording was grainy. The burglar stood in the entrance and looked around. Then he went directly to the glass box, opened it, and removed Boba Fett. Car headlights passed through the shop right at this moment, shining a light on the burglar's face. Georgie pressed pause. The long hair was not brown, but grey.

It wasn't Felicia. It was Udo.

Udo had worked at the shop for years. He went to high school with Uncle Jen and was never very bright. After he got hit by a mail truck, he really wasn't very bright. He lived in a small studio alone on the other side of town. He came in part-time mostly out of charity from Uncle Jen. He did some stocking and cleaning but never worked the cash registers. He seemed loyal to Uncle Jen and the shop and had never taken so much as a pog. Udo must have made a copy of his shop key before returning it to Georgie the previous week. Georgie would have never guessed in a million years that Udo was capable of such a caper.

Georgie sat back on the stool. He knew Udo's phone number but he didn't want to talk to him. He didn't want to call the police, either.

That afternoon, the shop was the quietest it had been in a long time. It seemed that with or without a large "Closing

Sale" sign outside, people just weren't that interested in obscure collectibles or weird toys or overpriced comic books. Maybe it wasn't that people in this town were cheap, maybe they didn't want what Georgie was selling.

Why couldn't Uncle Jen have had his own optometry practice or advertising agency or Michelin-starred restaurant? Then Georgie could have started working there during high school, and by now, he'd have a real profession and promising future in front of him. Instead, he was stuck in this stupid old shop surrounded by dusty plastic relics and the only people he interacted with were kids and strange adults and he finally had one opportunity to pursue a real relationship with a great woman and he blew it. For Beanie Babies.

Georgie began packing the items he knew would not sell before end of business Friday. Some would go in storage, others would be thrown away.

As the sun started to set, Georgie finally saw a FedEx truck appear through the window. It parked across the street. Felicia got out. She was in her usual blue cap and shorts and work boots. Georgie went to the window and knocked on the glass but Felicia didn't hear or see him. She unloaded some boxes from the back of her truck and stacked them onto a metal dolly before going inside the Old Sole Leather Shoe Repair store.

Georgie opened the shop door and went outside. He tried to look casual as he waited on the sidewalk, leaning against the side of his building. He could catch her coming out. He wanted to apologize of course, and maybe explain why he was acting the way he was, and perhaps try to turn it into a compliment. Felicia was so smart and athletic that he really thought she could be a master thief. Whatever he was going to say, he just wanted a chance to say it.

As Georgie waited, a husky man in a blue hooded sweatshirt and baseball cap came down the street and casually jumped into the back of the FedEx truck, disappearing from sight. But he wasn't a FedEx employee. Was he? No, thought Georgie. He didn't seem like one.

Georgie watched for cars then crossed the street. He circled around to the back of the FedEx truck.

The husky man was putting small boxes into a large nylon duffel bag when Georgie appeared.

"Excuse me," said Georgie. "What are you doing?"

The man zipped close his bag and turned around. Without a word, he ran toward Georgie and exploded out of the truck like a strong safety, knocking Georgie to the ground. The man lost no momentum as he bounced up from the pavement and sprinted off down the street holding his bag.

Georgie rubbed his shoulder. He watched the husky man turn onto Fundy Lane.

Then Georgie got up and ran after him.

Georgie lifted his knees and swung his elbows like he was taught in school as he ran down the sidewalk. The husky man was getting away. Georgie would have to be faster than he normally was if he had any chance of catching him. He turned the corner of Fundy Lane and caught a glimpse of the blue hooded sweatshirt just before the man vanished around the corner onto Bengal Lane.

Georgie picked up the pace.

Georgie was sweating and his bad knee was throbbing but he thought about how many boxes were in that man's bag and how many people would be unhappy if he got away. Georgie passed Family Time Beer and Liquor and PhoNomenal. People outside turned to see what the commotion was, first of the husky man running with the duffel bag then a few seconds later of Georgie huffing and puffing in hot pursuit.

When Georgie turned onto Biscay Lane, he lost sight of the man. But as Georgie ran toward the PennyMart, a few onlookers recognized what was happening and shouted and pointed Georgie in the right direction.

The chase continued through the main square. Georgie was already lightheaded but he recognized a few people in his blurry periphery as he entered the crowded center of town.

There was the Lima Boy with a group of his twerp friends. "Go get him, Georgie!" shouted the Lima Boy.

"You owe me twenty-five dollars!" shouted Georgie in return.

Then he passed Miss Wong outside of the post office.

She yelled, "Bring Veronica home in one piece!"

Georgie gave a thumbs-up and continued on past the Irish Pub. He saw Mr. Cadbury on the patio who jumped up excitedly. "Alright, Georgie!" yelled Mr. Cadbury. "I'll go get my gun!"

Georgie gave an emphatic *No, don't do that* wave and Mr. Cadbury sat back down. Georgie was confident. He could take care of this bastard all by himself.

The husky man went down the steps toward City Hall. As Georgie followed him, he thought maybe there was an opening. He was close enough. He could see the man's hair color and the texture on his sweatshirt. Georgie knew these steps well. He used to train on them years ago every Sunday with his ultimate Frisbee team. Georgie stepped up onto the metal hand railing at full speed and launched his body out into the cool spring air, through an invisible cloud of fruit flies, across several steps, landing only halfway on the back of the husky man. Packages went flying out of the duffel bag and Georgie held on for dear life as both men tumbled to the bottom of the steps.

The man's body ended up right on Georgie's leg, but Georgie managed to roll him off and get on top of him. He pulled back his hood to reveal him.

It was a man Georgie had never seen before. He was not from this town.

As Georgie struggled to hold him down, bystanders arrived to help and soon there was a small gathering of people watching from the top of the steps.

The crowd cheered and someone even whistled.

Georgie let go of the man and rolled onto his back, wheezing. He thought he might throw up.

When the police came, they took away the cat burglar and offered Georgie a ride to the hospital. Someone from the newspaper asked Georgie a few questions and even snapped his picture before he left the scene.

In the hospital that night, a nurse told Georgie that the police went to the husky man's motel room and found more stolen merchandise, from golf clubs to laptops to Persian rugs to a creepy airline stewardess mannequin. He was, it seems, the cat burglar in town. Georgie left the hospital on crutches.

Friday morning finally came. When Georgie got to the shop, a few high school kids were smoking pot again out front but Georgie didn't chase them away.

There was a note glued to the front door of the shop. Georgie read it before going inside.

My dear Georgie boy,

Sorry I stole your Beanie Babies. I will pay you back one day! Pinky swear. But I needed money for my medicines. Maybe if you start a new business one day you can hire me. I won't do it again! Please tell the others—I am NOT the cat burglar! I only stole from you. You are a good man and Uncle Jen is smiling at us I think.

Sincerely yours,
Udo

P.S. Thank you for the final paycheck!

The moving company came and took away most of the boxes. There were only a few that Georgie wanted to keep himself. A lot of people came by to wish him good luck and to ask for more details about the cat burglar. Someone gave Georgie a newspaper. He was on page four.

After lunch, Georgie cleaned out the backroom. He tore down all of the lists on the wall including his own, *Like a Champion Last Acts*. Georgie checked off each item. As he disassembled the Bowser Hog Island train track, he found a new list he had never seen before. It was hidden inside the tiny central station. It was titled *Patrons of Pot* and written on it were things like *Gregory – Dime Bag – Paid* and *Betty's Kid – Quarter Ounce – 20 Hours of Yard Work* and *Moe – Whole Ounce – Still Unpaid!*

So Uncle Jen had a little help all these years, thought Georgie, smiling. He threw away the incriminating list and finished disassembling the train track.

The door jingled and Felicia walked in. She waited by the entrance until Georgie came out from the backroom.

"Hi," said Georgie.

"Your leg," said Felicia.

"It'll heal," said Georgie, limping. "I'm really glad you decided to come by."

"I didn't want to after the other night," said Felicia. "But I thought I should say thank you for catching that crook and getting my packages back. You really saved my ass."

"About the other night," said Georgie.

"I don't want to talk about that now," said Felicia. "Besides, I don't have much time." She held out something for Georgie. "I just wanted to return this."

It was Icy the Beanie Baby.

"That was a gift," said Georgie.

"You should get to keep at least one of your Beanie Babies. And anyway, I'm not giving it back. I'm trading it."

"I see. And what exactly did you have your eye on?"

"Oh, one of those lovely *Predator* dolls, the big ones. They look way better than this sea otter. To be honest, I hated it the moment you gave it to me. But my dog liked it."

"You drive a hard bargain. But deal." Georgie took the Beanie Baby. "I just have to find Mr. Predator in one of these boxes."

"What will you do with all of them?" asked Felicia, looking at the remaining boxes.

"I'll start selling some things on eBay, just to get by the next months. You've got to change with the times, right? And it'll give me a chance to sell to people all over the world, not just this town. That should count for something."

"Certainly." Felicia looked down at her watch. "Well, I really do need to get back to work."

"Right, Mills," said Georgie.

"One of these days I'll be on time." Felicia opened the door to leave, then paused in the doorway. "Say, what was the name of that new coffee place you wanted to go to?"

"Bean There Done That," said Georgie.

Felicia smiled. "I'll see you around, Georgie."

The door closed and the shop was empty again. Georgie watched Felicia climb into her FedEx truck and drive away into town. Georgie sat at the main counter and rested his leg on the stool with the little sunflower pillow on the seat of it. He looked around. The shop seemed so much smaller now. Georgie placed Icy the Beanie Baby up on the counter with him. As he looked at it again, he noticed that it was pretty dirty on both sides and the heart-shaped tag had been chewed clean off. It was okay, thought Georgie. He wasn't going to sell it. Georgie sat there in the shop a few more hours that afternoon, enjoying the silence, watching people pass outside, thinking about all the things he wanted to do in the coming days and weeks and months and years, the sun gradually going down, his fluffy white seal with hopeful eyes watching him the whole time.

PIGS AND STOCK BOYS

Their eyes are on me. They know, sure they do. These Longs Drugs pigs and stock boys will fry my ass. *Pigs*, I got that from a James Cagney movie. I wasn't supposed to watch it, but I snuck down into the basement late and kept the volume real low. My dad would fry my ass if he knew I watched that *Goddamn* movie when he told me not to. Fry my ass worse than these *Goddamn* Longs Drugs pigs and stock boys.

There are mirrors up high, near the ceiling. Tilted, facing us at an angle, reflecting our ugliness back down to us like God. Running all the way around the store, one long horrific mirror. Like the command deck of some spaceship. What's behind the mirror? Aliens perhaps, pressed against the glass, breathing hot, studying the shopping behaviors of a cruel and hurtful species. Or maybe a floor of security analysts and intelligence specialists, dozens, *hundreds* of them, wired in, logging suspicious activity, speaking into headsets, direct messages to Washington. Facial recognition software. Speech pattern analysis. Brown ties.

Nothing can escape the Longs Drugs tilted mirror.

Do they know? Sure they do.

These Longs Drugs pigs will fry my ass.

I walk down Aisle B. Condoms and feminine products. Less suspicious or more suspicious? Buying a few things for mother, I'll say. Fewer questions. Very good. I linger by the ointments then move on to Aisle F, tools and home repair. Dad hasn't repaired a thing in years. The House of Wobbly Nuts and Protruding Nails. The whole town knows our place is a dump. Perhaps that makes it a harder story to sell, should the fuzz ask. Mom needs rubbers for when she sneaks out on dad, that's better. More believable? I cut back toward Aisle B. The linoleum squeals beneath my tennis shoes.

I'm only killing time. I always walk around before leaving. It's not illegal until you leave. That's where these dingbats screw it up. They flee in a rush, shaking like a leaf. Better to hang around awhile. *Yes, but I'm still shopping, sir. That's right, ma'am, this pack of baseball cards is in my pocket—but there were no shopping baskets available.* Then again, perhaps all shoplifters, deep down in their heart of hearts, want to get caught. Like serial killers who return to the scene of the murder. Gamblers who won't stop until they lose it all.

In fifty years, I believe all we'll have are trading cards, archives of what our society found important enough to print on rectangles of glossy cardboard. Upper Deck, WWE, Fleer, Pokémon, Marvel, *Batman Forever* Warner Brothers official premiere edition. The internet will burn, all cyberspace records with it. Future civilizations will wonder why we worshipped like gods Barry Sanders and Wonder Woman and The Macho Man Randy Savage.

In my pocket, while I walk, the thin foil around the pack of Topps Rookie Sensation MLB cards crackles. There was a special today. Free 99. Five Finger Discount. Everything must go.

I don't like baseball. Me and my old man used to watch Dodgers games every Saturday but that was before. Since his hours got reduced, the only activities he enjoys are drinking and shouting, sometimes together. Which I don't understand. He has more free time but spends less of it with us. Every Thursday evening when mom goes line dancing with her coworker, he leaves the house to play cards and get drunk with his friends. They work half days now, too.

Only a few more hours.

A Longs Drugs stock boy sees me. Aisle G, candy and junk food. Very suspicious, me pacing around there. *Damn.* Bush league mistake. Worst place for a good-for-nothing punk like me to be seen. Should have went to garden supplies. Stock boy might escalate this to pig. His walkie-talkie burps in robot. I smile uneasily then continue toward the checkout counter. Enough with these games, I need to blow this joint.

I head toward the sunlight.

The chief Longs Drugs pig stands guard by the door. He's fat and sweaty like a pig, but brown, not pink. I once read that security guards look for people who don't want to be seen. So I always make eye contact and stay in plain view. Right in front of their little snouts.

There's one open checkout counter. Five shoppers line up, all mothers of this town, but not like mine. They are homemakers, they buy groceries, they make sandwiches. I squeeze behind them, the only way to exit if you're not buying anything. I lock eyes with the pig. He stares back, then glances down at my pants. The foil wrapping must be sticking out of my pocket.

I walk faster.

I begin to tremble terribly. God, what was I thinking. I was too arrogant for coming today, especially after last time. Last time was really close. This was stupid. I should walk back and return the cards. It's too late. Dad will *really* fry my ass if I get caught. Mother will lose it. Send me to grandma's in Riverside like she always threatens she will. This time, dad will raise more than his voice. Better me than mom. Even when she's screaming and mean. Then again, maybe if I get caught, things will change. They will have to come get me together. They will apologize for not seeing this coming. They will say sorry for letting it get to this.

Tears are on the brink. The eyes of this pig, this Longs

Drugs security guard, burn a hole through me. He can see through my soul. The edges of my eyelids begin to burn, too. Spontaneous combustion is a real thing. I read it.

Turn away, stupid pig! Leave me alone. Get a real job, won't you? You don't need to ruin *my* life. Just because you have no friends, no family, probably no one on this Earth that loves you, it doesn't give you the right. Doesn't give anyone the right.

I walk a straight line, past the security guard, past his eyes, past his folded arms, past his pepper spray.

I make it. The pig is behind me.

Then it comes. "Hey, kid."

The first tear forms. A single warm drop, hanging from a leaky faucet, disobeying gravity, the first in a long stream of drops that will fall in this lifetime. Dad says only girls cry. But I saw him cry once. Drinking in the living room one night when mom was staying with a friend. My stomach tightens, my throat dries up.

"Doesn't Miss Ramsey know how to sew?" The security guard points down at my blue jeans, hand-me-downs from my cousin in Sacramento who I only met once. "Those holes are the size of bottle caps. Your money's going to start falling in the street, and I'm going to be the one to pick it up. Is that what you want, son?"

"No, sir," I say. "My mom will go shopping this week-end. She's buying me brand new jeans from Nordstrom."

He chuckles. "Nordstrom? Well, alright."

I leave Longs Drugs.

Outside, the sun is hot. I take out my pack of baseball cards and go toward the wooden-barrel trash cans. I see Hank, from the other class, unlocking his yellow Mongoose, holding a Longs Drugs plastic bag. He bought stuff.

"Hey, Hank," I say. "You like baseball?"

Hank pauses. Kids in the smart class are wary of my kind.

I hand him the pack. Hank smiles, caution fading, as he rips into the baseball cards. He rewards me with a Baby Ruth from his bag. Then he rides away, toward home, toward sandwiches.

I finish the chocolate bar and wipe my mouth. My body feels good. Nourished. I get on my bike and start riding in the other direction. I've got time. More time out here on these streets. I must go home eventually, but not now. Not yet. I have more time to lead these goddamn pigs a little farther, let them chase me a little longer. I am James Cagney. I am Joe Montana. I am the Joker, head out the window of a cop car, siren blaring, wind roaring. I am free just a little longer. Free as a bird. An eagle, American. When I return, mom will be dancing in the living room. Dad will be happy drunk, funny and buzzing. They will be in love and I will be their son. Until then, I will roam this Earth, pedal my Huffy like hell toward the horizon, sun against my back, sustenance in my belly, and nothing, not a thing can hold me back, not my parents, not these teachers, not this town, and certainly not these Longs Drugs pigs and stock boys.

Credits

"Ambrosia" | Published in *Cooper Street*

"Squirrels" | Published in *The Collapsar* (titled: "The Longhorns")

"Like a Norwegian" | Published in *Fjords Review*

"Gory Special" | Published in *Pithead Chapel*

"Bathroom Break" | Published in *Forth Magazine*

"The Long Weekend" | Published in *Tethered by Letters*

"Hansaring" | Published in *WhiskeyPaper*

"The Tenderloin" | Published in *East Bay Review*

"Be Sweet and Loving" | Published in *Stockholm Review*

"Park with Pops" | Published in *Saturday Night Reader* (titled: "Parking Cars")

"Rhubarb Pie" | Published in *Bookends Review Best of 2014* Anthology

"Pigs and Stock Boys" | Published in *PANK*

For many good reasons, thank you Leland, Melissa, Verena, Henriette, Lori, James Dickey, Eric, Kavinh, Brandon, Ryan, Daren, Alex, Cheung, Warren, GOC, Dan, Derrick, Scott, Steve, Weezy, Mark, Jon, Thea, Matt, Mike, Moritz, Bastian, Tim, Philipp, Beate, David, Fabio, Shamala, Janty, Pia, Leesa, Lindsey, Ben, Jimin, Kira, Lucy, William and Ruby.

Vincent Chu was born in Oakland, California. His fiction has appeared in *PANK Magazine, East Bay Review, Pithead Chapel, Fjords Review, Cooper Street, Stockholm Review, Chicago Literati, WhiskeyPaper* and elsewhere. He has been nominated for the Pushcart Prize and Sundress Publications Best of the Net. This is his debut collection. He wrote most of the stories in Cologne, Germany. He can be found online at vincentchuwriter.com and @herrchu.

7.13
BOOKS

Coleman Northwest
Regional

CPSIA information can be obtained
at www.ICGtesting.com
Printed in the USA
LVOW03s1555030418
572132LV00003B/728/P